Killa Season II
The Purge
by
Sa'id Salaam

Purge/PerJ/v.tr. 1. Make physically or spiritually clean. 2. Remove by cleaning. 3. Rid an organization, party, society of persons regarded as undesirable. 4. Empty bowels.

Prologue

"Who are you?" Doc demanded to know from the unknown stranger as he walked into the room. He was already hot about being snubbed by Killa and wasn't in the mood for company.

"I am the Chief of Police in San Jose, Costa Rica. I believe you know my daughter," the chief replied in a dangerous tone as he produced the jar containing her severed head from the bag that he carried. The bag also contained tools for torture and murder. It was about to get very ugly in there.

"Hey that's mine!" Doc shouted upon seeing the head in the jar.

"Huh?" the cop asked in confusion. "This is my daughter!"

"Well your daughter had such good head that I decided to keep it," the doctor shot back.

The Chief was furious and crossed the room to attack. Dropping the bag, which contained knives, scissors, duct tape, etc...all the party favors a killer needs, the furious father attacked from pure rage.

Doc was just plain crazy so it was a good match. The two fifty something year old men punched, kicked, and clawed to the death. It was evenly matched until the chief made a lunge for the bag. Doc was smart enough to know the bag contained his death and went for it too. They fought over the contents until one came up with a knife.

"Die!" Doc screamed as he plunged the huge blade into the man's mouth. It passed through his tonsils, throat, and brain before exiting out the back of his head. His eyes fluttered in good bye as his life slipped away.

Doc let go of the knife and watched the man fall to the floor. He was covered in blood from his head down to his pink erection. Murder had that effect on him; it always turned him on. The pretty, black woman who lured him there would have been nice, but she was gone already. Luckily, Bonita was still there; part of her anyway.

"Well hello Miss Bonita," Doc smiled flirtatiously at the head in the jar. They had a one sided conversation that ended up with her agreeing to give him some head; since that was actually all she had left anyway. She didn't really say yes, but she didn't actually say no either. Dead people tend to be indecisive like that.

Doc removed her head from the jar and inserted his penis into her opened mouth. With his nasty ass. Once he finished he put it back in the solution to keep it preserved. Then he showered, dressed, and prepared to embark on his next mission in life.

"Sold me out huh buddy?" he asked rhetorically to Killa, who was no longer present. "I'll show you who the real killer is. I'm coming for you now!"

Chapter 1

"I'm gon' get some pussy. I'm gon' get some pus-say!" Killa sang as he danced his way to the bedroom.

He had just put little Rico down for a nap and Xavier had fallen asleep playing video game. Both kids asleep at the same time meant one thing...

"I'm gon' get some pussy! Pus-say, oh yeah!"

"Yes you are mister man," Sincerity said as he entered the bedroom and spread her legs so he could enter her as well.

Killa dove face first between her thick thighs. The second his tongue touched her love button one of his phones began to ring. Most phones would get ignored at a time like this. You ever see a honeybee stop eating honey just because a phone rang? No, you have not!

It wasn't just any phone though. It was the satellite phone used only by family. When it rang, the world stopped spinning. His old business phone used to have that effect, but it hadn't rung since he blew Caspar into bite-sized pieces. He meant that literally since birds had come and gotten chunks to take back to their young.

The phone was supposed to be used for emergencies only but lately Grandma Diedra had lost track of what an actual emergency was. For instance, the day before she used it because the manager at the grocery store had taken cheese off sale. Her beloved granddaughter was coming home from school and she wanted to cook her famous macaroni and cheese.

"So what do you want me to do?" Killa had asked in confusion.

"Kill him," the old lady grumbled. It was a sign. A neon billboard sign that it was time to go. Time to pack up his family and leave the country.

Killa and his Dope Boy cousin had purchased a nice plot of land in South America. Houses for the entire family were being built right on the beach. It was time to retire and live. Only question was if they would live long enough to make it down there.

"Hello?" Killa answered in a 'what now' tone of voice that Diedra noticed immediately. She did raise him after all.

"Don't hello me! I need you to come over here right this minute!" she huffed indignantly.

"What the mailman put too many circulars in your box? Or did the bus driver said good morning after noon?" he teased.

"No, somebody shot my taxi up! Almost killed my grandbaby and me. Poor girl over here shaking like a leaf," Diedra relayed. She grossly misunderstood Cameisha's shaking. The girl was mad not scared. She wanted to march up the block and put a bullet in E-man's fitted cap for shooting at her.

"I'm on my way," he said and hung up.

Sincerity watched curious, as he got dressed and armed. "What's wrong baby?" she moaned and sat up straight.

"Somebody shot my grandmother's car up!" he replied.

"Yolo?" Sincerity shrieked in terror. The baby-cooking lunatic still unnerved her. She had been right there in her apartment holding her newborn.

"I told you she's dead. I shot her twice in the head."

"Oh yeah, after you fucked her," Sincerity spat back crossing her arms over her chest and twisting her face.

"Well you asked..." he reminded her.

She did, but she didn't expect him to say yes. One thing about Killa was he was brutally honest. Don't ask him something if you don't want to know.

"Anyway, her and my niece are fine," he said over his shoulder as he left out.

Killa casually crossed the courtyard with his gun in hand. It's not like anyone was going to call the cops on him. It's not like the cops were coming if someone did. Hell, even if they did come, they would have left him alone once they saw him. Killa only killed bad people and ain't nothing wrong with that.

"Are you ok?" he asked as he inspected his grandmother for bullet holes.

"Yes, but that sweet man who drove us..." Diedra mourned.

Cameisha stood up, twisted her lips, and cocked her head. Grandma got a kick out of watching them size each other up.

"Xavier this is Cameisha. Cameisha, say hello to your uncle," she demanded.

"Hello to my uncle," she spat sarcastically. Killa stifled a smile since he knew what was eating her. Sincerity had told him all about the feisty girl. Grandma was about to check the rude behavior until she spoke up in explanation. "I can take care of myself!"

"I'm sure," he said laughing at her mini-tantrum. The little murder-mami face was a good look, but... "I got this. Who was it?"

Cameisha crossed her arms defiantly and clenched her lips. It was body language for "I ain't telling you shit!" As soon as the sun set, she was walking two blocks over and putting two in his block head.

"You better tell him!" Diedra hissed. Both grandkids in attendance grew wide-eyed at the tone they knew so well.

"E-man, from 164th," she said stomping her foot and getting another stern look from Grandma.

"That bi...um...dude shooting at people," he wondered aloud. He and E-man grew up at the same time in that same section of the Bronx. That technically made them allies, but they were never friends.

Most dudes hated the pretty boy, who got all the girls, simply because he was a pretty boy who got all the girls. It was almost as if he was designated to pop all cherries in High Bridge. The whole hood got his sloppy seconds.

Killa hated him behind one particular cherry. He had the biggest crush on Puerto Rican Marcia on Davidson but was so busy trapping and busting guns, he couldn't get up with her. By the time he made time, it was too late. She was knocked up by E-man. Killa was crushed.

He couldn't kill him for that, but he could kill him for what he had now done.

"And just why is he shooting at you two?" he wondered.

Again, Cameisha paused until prodded by Grandma. Killa tried not to laugh as she laid out the whole story. Diedra snickered into her handkerchief at the tale of robbery and revenge. The story ended with his grandmother being shot at which meant E-man was getting shot.

"A'ight, I'll go holla at him," Killa announced. What that meant, was go murder him. He kissed his grandma and traded another once over with his niece. They both turned their noses up at each other like the other stank. It was some killer shit that killers do.

Killa had just entered the stairwell when he heard the apartment door open and close. That sound was quickly followed by quick steps in his direction. Running up behind Killa was usually a closed casket affair but he knew who it was. Expected her actually.

"Wait for it..." he laughed as she got closer, "...no!"

"Come on Unc, please! I should have murdered him last time. Please let me kill him," Cameisha pleaded sounding like a kid. Except she was begging to kill someone instead of asking for a Happy Meal. Then her big brown eyes filled with tears and she broke down into sobs.

"I lost my daddy and my granddaddy, please, please, please" she wailed desperately.

Killa didn't buy it for a second. "Fuck outta here," he cracked up at the transparent display.

Just as quickly, the waterworks stopped and she regained her composure. "Come on Unc, this is my beef. Let me handle it. I was taught by the best, let me finish this nigga!"

"A'ight, yo," Killa relented, moved by the reference of his beloved uncle. He was the best and if he taught her, she could handle it. "Just don't tell Grandma!"

****

The murder had to wait until after 10pm since that was Diedra's bedtime. Cameisha donned her bag lady camouflage and crept outside to meet her uncle.

"Really! You just gon' walk around like that?" she asked seeing the fifty caliber Desert Eagle in his hand.

"Who's gonna stop me?" he asked. No one with that thing in his hand. "A bag lady huh?"

"Shit works. Don't believe me, dig Tovia up, and ask her."

"I'll just take your word for it. Check it, walk up University, and I'll flush them to you. Be ready because they'll be coming fast."

"Flush 'em to me? Who you supposed to be?" Meisha laughed.

"I'm the boogie man. You ain't heard?" he replied seriously and turned on his heels. Killa marched over to Ogden Ave and bust a right towards 164th Street.

A police car cruising up the block cruised right by the armed man. The cops turned their heads as if they didn't even seen him and he kept right on marching. He was spotted again by a look out once he got to 165th. The kid took off running to alert the boss.

"Killa is coming!" he screamed as he burst through the doors of the pizza shop that served as E-man's headquarters. The words were still in the air when he ran out just as quickly.

A few more drug dealers scattered in all directions. Those closest to E-man stayed as long as he did. He was the boss after all.

"Who? A-yo fuck Killa! I'm a killer. He come up in here and I'ma slap a spark out his ass," E-man declared while standing. He took one last bite of pizza and announced, "I was 'bout to leave anyway."

As soon as he reached the sidewalk, he came face to face with Killa. Only, he didn't slap a spark out of him, didn't say fuck him to his face either. Instead, he screamed like a bitch and ran like a girl. When the boss took off running his workers did too. Right towards the bag lady.

The dirty bag lady smiled a bright, clean smile when she saw her target rushing towards her. The cans in her bag rattled loudly as she dug inside. She waited until he was right on top of her before pulling the Mac-10. A three shot burst into his torso made him dance causing his cronies to come to a skidding halt and turn back around.

"This kid," Killa sighed when his niece bent over to talk to the wounded man. He couldn't hear what was being said and couldn't worry about it. Not with his crew running straight in his direction. He raised the cannon and fired off four quick shots. The men looked like acrobats as the heavy slugs had them turning flips and somersaults.

Cameisha finished her talk and put six in his face. Both killers left the same way they came, and met back in the project's courtyard.

"See! I told you I was dope!" Meisha cheered and raised her hand for a high five.

Killa left her hanging in mid-air. "Amateur," he chuckled and walked off. She was dope, but cocky. If she didn't shake that trait, it would be her downfall. And in her profession, it meant the difference between an open or closed casket.

****

"Did you guys have fun?" Sincerity asked in just above a whisper when Killa returned. That meant the kids were asleep and that meant it was about to go down.

"Huh?" he asked since her nakedness stole his sense of hearing. He wouldn't need it anyway.

Sincerity slinked over and knelt before her king. She moved his erection from his pants and into her mouth before the air could touch it. The couple flipped into 69 as if performing a ballet. They took each other orally right to the brink and stopped.

She mounted him like he was a horse. A short ride later, they both arrived at their destination. Both were too tired to move so neither did. They fell asleep right there in that position on the plush living room carpet. That's where they woke up too early the next morning. Awoke to little Xavier's cartoons and him right above them on the sofa.

Chapter 2

"What the fuck?" Killa asked the ringing phone that should not have been ringing. The only people who had the number were dead and he was almost certain they didn't have phones where he sent them. Casper was in a hundred pieces, so no way was he calling.

"What's wrong honey?" Sincerity asked seeing the mask of confusion on his face. If she didn't know the fearless man as well as she did she would have sworn she saw fear in his brown eyes.

"Nothing," he said regaining that exclusive South Bronx swagger as he picked up the phone and casually took the call.

"Hey bae. It's me, Yolo, or should I say yo' baby mama? How crazy is it that since the last time we saw each other we were trying to kill each other. And we ended up doing it," Yolo giggled, paused, and then continued. "So anyway I was watching Animal Planet, Shark Week is my favorite, but they had big cats. I wish I could have a lion. Anyway, I learned when a lion takes over a pride, that's a pack of lions you know? I didn't know that, but anyway, when a lion takes over a pride he kills all the baby lions so the girl lions will go into heat and only have little lions from his loins. Lion, loins, that's funny..."

"You're dead...I killed you," Killa said recalling firing into the back of her head, not once but twice. Right after he came in her.

"Nuh uh, my wig was bullet proof silly! Anyway I'm in Philly waiting on little Xavier so I can kill him. Then Rico and his mama, so our child and I will be your only concern. No baby mama drama for us."

"Listen" Killa began slowly and calmly. He knew full well he was dealing with a lunatic. Sure, he killed a bunch of people, but this chick was fucking crazy. "I need to meet you so we can..."

"Oops, gotta go! Talk to you later, bye-bye," Yolo sang and clicked off the line. She was only midway through Jersey and still had a ways to go to get to Philly.

Killa rushed from the apartment with nothing more than a cell phone and pistol. Divine decree cleared his path of roadblocks and cops as he raced south towards Philadelphia. He arrived in record time, which was just in time to see his beloved first born murdered in front of his eyes.

Little Xavier had just stepped out of the schoolhouse when his father came to a skidding stop. The father smiled at his son as he approached and got a friendly smile in return. That's when Yolo pulled the trigger exploding his head with a high-powered slug.

"No!" Killa roared like a lion at the sight of his dead cub at his feet. A curious crowd began to gather instantly cutting the wanted man's mourning short. He had no choice but to slip away once the sirens drew near.

Killa tapped out a quick text that sent his family back into hiding. Grandma Diedra met Sincerity and sons in the courtyard and they disappeared to one of Killa's many safe houses. Meanwhile, he shot over to Germantown where he kept a rented room.

His plan was to plot his next move, but images of his son's murder kept replaying in his mind like a bad movie. He could still see the smile on his face as he left this world for the next. His only solace was knowing that his innocent child was in paradise with the prophets.

Killa sat for hours in the window watching life unfold on the street below. The call to prayer resonated from a nearby masjid and snapped him from his thoughts. He nodded his head in agreement at the phrase God is the greatest. Even though he didn't speak Arabic, the heart translates the phrase and brings peace. It was one of the few times in his violent life that he was at peace. However, it wouldn't last.

"Bitch!" a loud-mouthed thug screamed as he slapped his cute girlfriend to the concrete sidewalk. The blow obviously wasn't abusive enough, so he delivered a short kick to her midsection.

"Not your business," Killa told himself out loud, as he shook his head at the sad display.

It was sad on so many levels. One, because this wasn't the first time. No, G-Money had been whipping Krystol's ass for quite some time.

They both had seen so much domestic abuse they both considered it to be the norm. Killa would have minded his business if G-Money hadn't opened his mouth and revealed the reason for the beating.

"Now you gon' take yo' ass down to that clinic and get that abortion! I should make yo' ass sleep out on the sidewalk so you can be first in line," G-Money shouted down at the cowering girl. "Just like I did when the new Jordans came out."

"They said I ain't gon' be able to never have a baby if I keep having all these abortions," Krystol whined from behind her arms that were raised to block his blows. "That's why they gave me all those condoms last time!"

"Bitch, I ain't wearing no damn condoms! Who the fuck you think I am?" he growled raising a hand to hit her again. "You just need to stop fucking getting pregnant!"

"Ok, ok, I'll have the abortion. Just please stop beating me," Krystol said giving up on yet another unborn child.

Killa had heard enough. For the man who just lost a child it was actually more than enough. Plus, he really, really wanted to kill someone to take the edge off. Some random somebody would have died if G-Money hadn't stepped up and volunteered. Killa grabbed his gun and headed outside.

Krystol climbed to her feet and fell in step behind her so-called boyfriend. He was a boy, but what kind of friend was that? She walked two steps behind him with her head lowered in submission. She stepped lightly as if actually walking on eggshells. Ironically, a Muslim couple walked by hand in hand laughing at another of her jokes. So much for that stereotype...

Killa followed casually at a distance as they walked along. G-Money thought it was cute to throw fake punches at the girl and giggled when she flinched. He was going to pay for that. When his prey slipped into the weed spot, the predator followed him inside. A gas pack always goes well with a murder.

A few blocks later, they reached a rundown row house. G-Money sent his woman inside with a swift kick in her ass. "Bitch, have me a sandwich ready when I get back. You know I can't blow no gas 'round Ma Dukes 'cause that bitch gon' be begging to hit the blunt! Free loading ass always want a pull or begging for some help with the bills. Fuck I look like paying bills in my own home?" he rambled and walked away with his murderer close behind. When they reached a nearby park, Killa introduced himself.

"Sup yo, match one?" Killa offered, showing the neatly rolled blunt he'd prepared as they walked.

"That's what's up! Only I um...left my sack at the crib. We can blaze yours and I'll run and get mine once we're done," G-Money greedily agreed.

"Cool and I'll just wait here for you," Killa said with faked wide-eyed nativity.

"Won't be but a sec," he replied, trying not to laugh at the sucker he lucked up on. "Fire that up!"

Killa leaned in and accepted the long flame from his lighter. He took a deep drag off the fruity herbs and felt his problems postpone till later. Some people use drugs as an escape when really, it's just a pause. All of your problems will still be waiting when you get back. He took one more and passed it off. He should have taken another because it wasn't coming back.

"Saw you putting the smack down earlier," Killa offered casually, leading him on.

"Yeah...my girl...keep...getting pregnant on me," he explained between pulls on the blunt and sips of air. "Plus she be talkin' stupid shit, talkin' about she wanna go to school and I need a job and..."

Killa let him ramble on and on, digging his own grave deeper with every syllable. The world may or may not be a better place without G-Money, but it was about to find out. Just when he figuratively reached six feet deep, he got a pass.

"Really, I believe she likes me to whoop that ass. If not, she would have left me right?" G-Money asked.

Of course, Killa had no reply to that. He hated that it almost sounded reasonable. Why would a woman stay with a man who abuses her mentally, verbally, or physically? Killa couldn't figure it out either so he gave him a pass on his life. It didn't last long though because G-Money opened his mouth again and the pass was snatched out of his hand.

"My moms too! Oh, I be having to smack her ass too. Stealing my weed clips out of the ashtray. Beggin' for help with the bills. Shit, she works, I don't! Pay your own bills bitch; I just stay there. See I'm from the smack-a-ho tribe. I'll smack a ho, any ho," he said tearing the pass into tiny pieces.

Killa just shook his head as the man smoked and dug. He dug his grave and smoked Killa's weed until it burned his fingertips. Only then, did he attempt to pass it back.

"Nah, I'm good," Killa said to the wet roach between his weed stained fingertips.

"A'ight, I'ma run and get my weed. Stay here, I'll be right back."

"Nah, you won't," Killa growled and pulled a gun.

G-Money turned to run but a slug spun him back around. The next shot dropped him and the one after that killed him. The next four were just because they felt good.

"Men are the protectors and maintainers of women!" Killa growled down at the corpse. Waste of breath really, because dead people are notoriously bad listeners.

Chapter 3

The weed and murder managed to get Killa's mind off his son, but only for a moment. They both provided a high, but once he came down, his issues still waited impatiently. To make matters worse, he had no idea where to even begin to look for the girl. And what the fuck was that pregnant talk? On a futile whim, he used the business line and tried to reach her. He wasn't able to track them through the phone before, and nothing had changed. The call went straight to voicemail where the goofy girl had left him a message.

"Hey babe, sorry I can't take your call right now," Yolo sang. She tried to sound professional, but broke into a giggle. "Don't worry honey, this will all be over soon, and we can live happily ever after. The three of us, just the three of us."

"Fuckin' lunatic," Killa growled and hung up without leaving a message. What was there to say anyway? Come meet me somewhere so I can murder you?

Killa flipped on the TV hoping to quell the growing rage. Watching black people make buffoons out of themselves on reality shows only made him angrier. The violent movies amused the violent man so he turned to the news. Talk about violence!

First was ISIS and their bullshit. As noble as creating an Islamic state might be, terrorism contradicts the tenants of faith and defeats the purpose. Then there was the usual black on black crime that black people love so much. The next story was even more violent and only served to infuriate the angry man.

A verdict had been reached in a Georgia murder trial. The case had polarized the nation and everyone awaited the outcome. Black people waited to see if it was still open season on young black men and white men hoped that it was. Slavery had long been abolished so this was all they had.

Black people often say, "I wish a nigga would," but not as much as some racist whites. They wished and prayed that a nigger would.

George Zeigler was one of them and he just got his wish. Ever since the day his home was burglarized, he had been waiting for the day to kill a black boy. That's despite the fact that it was a couple of white kids in the neighborhood who broke in.

They received slaps on their wrist and their parents were required to pay restitution. Besides, who kills little white kids except other white kids? He was too old to shoot up a high school, so instead he loaded up on guns and waited and wishing a nigger would. To that end, he would drive away; park his car, and sneak back to his house, hoping for a burglar.

"Huh?" George asked as he watched a baseball sail over his fence into his backyard. He assumed, correctly, that it belonged to the black kids who played baseball one street over. He had dubbed them the Negro league, and they were not getting their ball back.

"Hello? Anyone home? Hello, we lost our ball!" 16-year-old Randall Martin called out as he popped his head over the wooden security fence. He scanned the yard looking for the ball and spotted it near the back door. Randall called out a few more times before hoisting himself over the fence.

"Yes!" Zeigler cheered pumping his racist fist. He cocked his gun and ran to greet his guest.

Just as the child bent to pick up the ball, the back door flew open. The startled teen stood up right into the line of fire, as George fired. The round from the .357 made a large hole in Randall's forehead and an even larger one in the back where it exited. The adult stood over the child and put another round through his stopped heart.

"Fuck you looking at nigger?" he asked the boy whose eyes were opened wide from the shock of being murdered. George chuckled proudly as he looked down at his handy work. He casually took a few pictures for souvenirs then calmly called the cops. As soon as the operator picked up, he put on a show.

"Yes, send help right away! I'm white and a black man tried to break into my home. I got off a couple of shots but there might be more of them!" he said convincingly.

"A black man," the operator gasped, "Stay put! Help is on the way!"

The 911 tape was played several times in the jury room, but it was just for show. The whole trial was just a farce to shut up the hollers of the black community. The powers that be could give a fuck about a dead black boy. If not for the uproar of blacks, George would have gotten a medal. In fact, he did get a plaque from the secret society he belonged to.

K.A.N.A.S. was an acronym for Kill All Niggers And Spics. Their hatred extended to Jews, Arabs, and normal white people who didn't share their racist attitudes. In their twisted view, if you didn't hate niggers, you had to be a nigger lover. The sick fucks.

Killa frowned knowingly at the screen as he watched the jury return. The foreman twisted his ring then smoothed his hair. The judge nodded ever so slightly and the DA did the same. The defense counsel stifled a smile at the good news.

"Y'all better not," Killa growled. He, like the rest of the country, followed the case enough to know the homeowner was a piece of shit who murdered a good kid. This was by all accounts, an open and shut case. A slam-dunk as they say.

"Has the jury reached a verdict?" the judge boomed down sounding all official and shit, with his corrupt ass.

"We have," the foreman replied smugly and handed the verdict sheet to the bailiff.

The bailiff shuffled it over to the judge. He frowned at it and passed it back. The process was reversed, and they were ready to publish the verdict for the world.

"As to count one, malice murder, how do you find?" the judge asked sucking all the air from the courtroom.

"Not guilty!" Michael O'Connor announced standing proudly as if the National Anthem was playing. The verdict set off an uproar in the packed court. Even still, the woeful moan of a grieving mother broke through.

"My baby," Mrs. Martin sobbed breaking Killa's heart. Her pain and anguish mixed with his own, and flushed a lone tear from his eye.

George and his attorney hugged triumphantly as the jury acquitted him on the rest of the felony charges as well. He was found guilty of a misdemeanor for not putting his garbage cans close enough to the curb. It was a subliminal snub that had the killer seeing red. The post-trial interview only made it worse

"Yes I'm just relieved this whole ordeal is behind me," George said with a sigh. "I'm ready to get some rest and back to my life."

"Poor George. Don't worry, Killa's coming to help you get some rest," Killa said soothingly. "I'm going to kill you, your lawyer, the crooked ass judge, and every last one of those jurors. You're all dead!"

Chapter 4

Killa spent a restless night in the rented room. Every time he closed his eyes he relived his child's murder. A blunt of the gas put him in a coma too deep for dreams. He was awakened just before the crack of dawn by the Muslims' call to prayer. Again, a tranquil peace descended upon his heart as he listened.

Prayer is better than sleep. God is the greatest; God is the greatest. There is nothing worthy of worship except God!

Again, he watched from his window as Muslims flocked from every direction to answer the call. After a few minutes of quiet contemplation, Killa got up, and got dressed so he could go kill some people who really, really needed killing.

A flight from Philly to Atlanta would have been both quicker and cheaper than driving, but Killa wanted to stay off the radar. One thing he did know was that the Black Mob was everywhere. He had no way of knowing if or how much of the structure remained in that after he killed the head.

His first stop in Georgia was to his new/old friend Big Shawn. He had fifteen people to kill and planned to have fun doing it. Sure, he could just shoot them all, but where's the fun in that? No, he planned to get creative. Speaking of fun, he waited until the wee hours of the night and broke in for old time's sake.

"What the..." Big Shawn asked as the aroma of cooking food snatched him awake. He shot a glance at his guest and saw she was still sleeping peacefully from the good pipe he had just laid.

Hell, even if she had been awake, she wouldn't be in the kitchen. The twenty something year old woman was too busy 'turning up' to learn to cook. She knew every new dance and the words to every new song, but ask her to fry an egg. Sex was the only thing she had to offer and Big Shawn took her up on it. He brought her home from the club and dicked her down.

Big Shawn slid from the bed as quietly as his creaking bones would allow. He reached between the mattress and box spring and grabbed a hammer. Not the kind of hammer people use to nail stuff with, but the kind people get nailed with. He slowly cocked the gun and followed his nose.

"I hope you like your eggs hard because that's how I scrambled them," Killa called out, letting Big Shawn know he heard his big toes tiptoeing towards him. That way, he wouldn't get shot.

"Aye yo, what the fuck are you doing in here?" Big Shawn asked letting the gun fall to his side.

"Just came to make breakfast," he replied nodding to the pile of turkey bacon, biscuits, and cheese eggs. "Don't worry, I made enough for little Miss Oh! Oh! Get it daddy, in there. I hope you used a condom 'cause I went through her phone and ma had more dick pics than the law allows."

"A condom? Shit, I used two! I just met shawty at the club. I don't think she eats anything but pills though," he said thoughtfully.

"And dick from what I saw when I came in. She's like a circus performer," Killa laughed. He then fixed the plates while his host poured orange juice. They sat down at the glass dinette table and dug in.

"So, what brings you to town?" Big Shawn inquired midway through the meal.

"The usual, gon' kill a few people," Killa said between bites.

"Anyone I know?" he asked offhandedly, since he could give a damn. He knew his guns killed people and never concerned himself with the why. Minding your own business was a part of the curriculum in New York schools. It should be a law.

"Actually, yes. You seen the Zeigler trial?"

"Yeah I saw that bullshit! A straight A, good kid, made out to be a thug. How did the jury even go for that lame ass shit? That's what I wanna know!" Shawn spit hotly.

"I'll ask them before I kill them. Judge too, the whole shit was fixed. How the fuck you get an all-white jury in a 60% black county? Add another 10% for Hispanics and 8% other and it adds up to some fuck shit," Killa said doing the math.

"Damn son! You're going to kill all of them? All 12, 13, um 16 people?" he asked, cocking his head dubiously.

"Yup, and whoever is with them, and whoever don't like it. You got a problem with that?"

"Problem? Shit no! I want in!" he shot back enthusiastically.

"You know I work alone. Well, for the most part," he said recalling letting his niece Cameisha ride along once. That was fun.

"Dude, 16 people! Let me get at least...three," Big Shawn asked making sure to leave a little room for negotiation.

"One," Killa relented seeing the eagerness in his eyes.

The rest of the country was holding rallies, making speeches, and other useless bullshit, but what America needed was a good purge, and it was about to get one. It's not like the racists would just get so tired of protests that they would stop killing black boys.

On the contrary, they would eventually kill every last one if all that would happen is people holding hands and chanting old Negro spirituals. Fuck that, an eye for an eye, funeral for funeral. We'll stop when you stop. I guess black men will have to stop killing each other first though...

"Well let's go shop. I got some new and exciting stuff," Big Shawn said and stuffed his last biscuit in his mouth.

Killa took two last forkfuls that emptied his plate and stood up behind him. He followed his host into the showroom and had the same reaction he always did. "Damn!" Killa exclaimed feeling lightheaded as all the blood rushed from his brain to his dick. The sight of all the guns and killing devices always gave him a hard on.

"You ok? I can send you in there with Mandy...uh, Miranda? Shit, I have no idea what that girl's name is. Something with an M? Anyway, just say 'turn up' and her legs spread quicker than a rumor," Shawn offered shaking his head. All that's going on and all the youth want to do is turn up.

"Nah, I'd rather make a few people turn up dead," he declined and picked up a sniper rifle.

He sat the long-range murder weapon on an empty table that wouldn't be empty for long. Big Shawn immediately added the silencer that went with it like the salesman that he was. Instead of fries with that shake, this was bullets for that gun? By the end of the excursion, the table was loaded with death. They were done until one last item caught Killa's eye.

"What...the...heck...is...that?" he had to know.

"That my friend is the D.C. 2000," Big Shawn proudly proclaimed. "A knock off actually, but works just the same."

"What does it do?" Killa inquired and once it was demonstrated, he said, "Damn!"

"I'll take it. How much for everything?" he asked reaching for his cash stuffed pockets.

"Since this is a noble cause it's on the house. Come on. I'll help you load this in the car. Or do you have a tank packed outside?" he laughed.

As soon as they stepped from the showroom, they came face to face with a very naked and very worried Malaysia. That's her name by the way. At least Shawn remembered the first letter.

"Where did you go?" she pouted. "When I woke up to pee-pee I didn't see you and I got confused."

Got confused, Killa wondered and got confused himself. The very pretty girl had a ton of make up over her skin and pounds upon pounds of weave piled on her healthy shoulder length hair. She even wore grey contacts on top of light brown eyes. The girl didn't just get confused; she's obviously been confused.

"I um, had to um, talk to my friend," Big Shawn stammered. The girl took a look at all of the guns and was about to panic. Luckily, he knew the magic words. "Turn up!"

"Hey!" Malaysia sang and raised her hands above her head. She closed her eyes and wound her hips to the music that always played in her head. It probably echoed in that big open space. The drugs and music had effectively lobotomized her and most of her generation.

While she was busy turning up, Killa and Big Shawn slipped outside with the guns. The dealer helped load them like a bag boy at the grocery store. Once they completed the task, they turned and faced each other.

"Aye yo, don't forgot me. Let me get at least one," Big Shawn reminded. It had been a long time since he got his hands dirty, but this was a great time to start again.

"I got you fam," Killa replied extending his hand. The men exchanged pounds and man hugs then Killa departed.

Malaysia was still turning up when Big Shawn returned. "Hey!" she sang as she danced and turned up. Big Shawn led her back to the room and turned her up doggy style on the bed. After rolling two condoms down his erection, he slid safely up inside her. Turn up!

Chapter 5

Juror number 12 aka Jane, was a very pretty, thirty something year old white lady. She had bright blonde hair, big fun breasts, and a small waist above her tight ass. She was comfortably married with a comfortable home, and a couple of children. Comfortable, but not happy because she was a selfish bitch who demanded more out of life and her husband than was written for her.

Juror number 5, John, was a wannabe rock star/cowboy type fuck up. He worked out religiously and had amassed more brawn than brains. He was busting at the seams with machismo and Jane liked machismo. John was too stupid to pass the police exam, so he had to settle for being a security guard. No gun, but at least he got a flashlight. It was the only bright thing about the man.

The two potential jurors saw the potential in each other during the jury selection process prior to the trial. The pool of one hundred was reduced to two when their blue eyes met from across the crowded room. She played coy, ducking her head, and batting her eyes. Meanwhile, he had one speed, full steam ahead. John flashed his smile and peered into her soul.

Once the blacks were eliminated for being black, the jury pool was reduced to twenty-five. A series of questions were asked to identify the liberal and progressive types. If you believed black people were people you were sent home as well. By the end of the day, the state had a jury they could count on. They could literally convict a ham sandwich with that bunch. Or, more importantly, acquit one. And that's exactly what racist George Zeigler was, a fucking ham sandwich.

Being numbers 12 and 5, they were separated in the jury box, but inseparable any other time. Although they were sequestered at the same hotel, there was too much going on to link up. They chatted, complimented, and flirted until it was clear they would eventually fuck. It was all a prelude to the pussy.

John didn't get much action being a gym-oholic and all around cornball. He had no problem attracting chicks, but always said some dumb shit that turned them off. Jane on the other hand, had regular affairs to break the monotony of her life.

After they let Zeigler off for murdering the black boy, they stayed in contact. They traded texts, emails, and finally naked pictures. She was impressed with his hard, hardly used dick, and he with her pretty, pink, parted labia.

Jane made dinner for her family and then made an excuse to leave them. John lived with his mom who twisted her lips dubiously when he announced he had a date.

"With a girl?" she cackled and snickered. All her son ever talked about was his gym buddies. Not to mention all of the muscle magazines full of oiled up muscle men.

"Ma I'm not gay!" he insisted stomping his feet like a 12 year old. He said it again to himself to be sure.

A single man alone with a married woman is never a good idea. Luckily, Killa was there to chaperone. He watched from across the restaurant as they dined on quesadillas and tequila. Even though he planned to make it public, this was a little too public. No one wants brain matter in their guacamole so he waited.

"Guess we should go fuck now?" Jane suggested once the meal was eaten.

"Only if I can get some brains too," John replied. He overheard the term in the gym and would love to run back and report getting some brains himself.

"My specialty!" Jane cheered truthfully.

The bill was paid and off they went. John couldn't take her home and his meager earnings forbid renting a hotel room. A local park was picked which was perfect for Killa. It was public. He found a spot in the tree line and assembled the sniper rifle.

"Nice!" Killa whispered as he peered through the night vision. It cast the couple in a bright green light just as Jane clocked in for her blowjob.

"Nice!" John exclaimed at his first blowjob in ages. Jane said something in reply, but her mouth was too full to make it out. Maybe, thanks for the compliment?

"Bye-bye juror number five," Killa said and squeezed the trigger. The round sped silently through the air, into the open window, and through John's head before lodging in a tree.

"Mm hmm," Jane said proudly feeling his body jerk. She continued sucking until it deflated in her mouth. "I could have stayed home if I wanted a limp dick!"

Jane's protest was cut short when she saw the hole in her date's head. She opened her mouth to scream but nothing came out. That was due to the slug going in. It came out of the back of her head leaving a hole big enough for her brain to fall out and into John's lap. Be careful what you wish for. He wanted some brains, and he got it.

****

Jurors 12 and 5 weren't the only ones to make a love connection. People tend to get close when confined together. Put strangers together for a long enough time and somebody's going to fuck.

Juror 1 was a tall, handsome man with a good job and quick wit. And so was juror number 2. The two men projected masculinity that concealed their inner bitch. They didn't even know they were gay until fate pushed it to the surface. Being sequestered they ended up sharing a hotel room. The first night they did everything but fuck. The second night they butt fucked. After the trial, they became a couple.

"Sho' nuff?" Killa giggled when he found out. The mass murderer could be quite silly at times and it tickled him immensely when he found out Adam and Steve were Adam and Steve.

He had followed the couple not knowing they were a couple into a midtown sports bar. He thought it a little odd when Steve giggled from a pat on the ass Adam gave when he made a difficult bank shot. After all, athletes pat each other on the ass every day. They don't usually giggle though. The lip-to-lip peck they shared after Steve sank the 8-ball pretty much summed it up.

Only then, did Killa glance around the establishment. He had been so focused on his prey he didn't even notice it was a gay sports bar. It was full of cowboys and Indians and studs and fems. The name on the sign suddenly made sense. "Man Down."

"Hey sailor, buy a girl a drink?" a petite sissy suggested climbing on the stool adjacent to his murderer.

"Beat it cocksucker," Killa growled in an attempt to spare him. Only the gay man who had unprotected sex with other gay men did not want to be spared. It was obvious he wanted to die. It was his unlucky day.

"That's Miss Cocksucker to you," he/she giggled and placed his hand on Killa's thigh.

"Dude, are you touching me?" Killa asked incredibly.

"I'm trying to give you some head," he pouted.

"You know what?" Killa said nodding thoughtfully. He wanted to see how the D.C. 2000 worked anyway. "I'll take you up on your offer, but I gotta warn you, you're not getting your head back."

"Oh a macho man!" the sissy giggled. He liked the homo-thug type that snuck around. He hopped off the stool ready to go.

Killa glanced over at his targets just in time to see a fresh pitcher of beer being delivered by a fairy, dressed as the tooth fairy, and knew he had a few minutes to spare. He stepped off the stool and led the way out of the bar.

"We can go to the pond," the sissy suggested of the park across the street. It was where a lot of gay men went for quick romps. Most were married or at least on the down low. Probably a couple of male urban fiction authors as well, but you didn't hear that from me.

"A'ight, let me grab something from my trunk," Killa agreed and made the slight detour. He grabbed the device and followed him into the park.

Killa wished he had a pair of blinders on to miss the man on man action on the benches. Even the slope leading to the pond was surrounded with men on their knees or hand and knees with other men inside them.

"Here we go," the sissy said dropping to his knees in front of Killa and reaching for his zipper.

"One sec, try this on," he said putting the gadget over his head.

"What is it?" he asked curiously. We all know that curiosity killed the cat. Killed this cat too.

"A cocksucker ring," Killa replied and hit the switch. The device snapped shut and popped his head off. It rolled down the incline and into the pond. "Told you, you wasn't getting it back."

Adam and Steve were walking out just as Killa returned. He rushed back to his own car and pulled out behind them. Once the coast was clear, he pulled up beside them at a light and pulled the pin.

"Excuse me?" Killa called politely hoping Steve would roll down his window. He did, but only halfway. Still, it was enough.

"Yes?" he asked with a 'what the hell do you want nigger' expression on his face.

"What's the quickest way to get to hell?" he inquired.

"Making partners with God?" Adam guessed correctly from the passenger seat.

"I was gonna say die, but that's a better answer! Anyways, bye-bye, time to die!" Killa said and tossed the grenade into the backseat. He mashed the gas pedal and watched in his rearview mirror. The blast turned the occupants inside out and flipped the car upside down.

Four jurors down, eight more to go, plus the judge, the prosecutor, defense attorney, and finally, the man of the hour George Zeigler himself. That way, he knew it was coming.

Chapter 6

Four jurors from a high profile case murdered in two days could not be ignored. The state ordered that the surviving jurors as well as the judge be placed in protective custody. The offer was extended to the prosecutor and defense attorney, who both declined.

George Zeigler was labeled a hero by his fellow K.A.N.A.S. members and provided around the clock security. The more the merrier; have Killa tell it.

A five star hotel was selected and for some reason, broadcast on the news. Perhaps they wanted to show how well the state treated its partisan juries. Convict an innocent person and eat prime rib and drink fine wine. All they really did was facilitate their own demise.

"Well gee, thanks!" Killa said to the news reporter lady when she made the announcement. They even showed the plush hotel's dining room, pools, and suites. He couldn't believe how easy they made it for him. It only took a few minutes of casing the joint before he found a way in.

Killa never liked serving anyone other than his family, but made an exception for the judge and jury. The corrupt judge jumped at the chance to see juror number 9 again. They discreetly flirted throughout the whole trial. She would wink her long fake lashes and blow kisses with her big fat Botox lips. She looked like a middle-aged Caucasian Lil Kim. And that's not good.

The judge would wink back and stroke his little erection under his robe. Why not since he didn't have to pay attention to the proceedings. Any time a white person was found guilty in his court, he made sure there was an error that would get it overturned on appeal.

Besides, the regular waiter was bound and gagged in the basement, so somebody had to serve the wine. That night, a special vino was poured just for their group. In fact, it had been manufactured just for them.

"Wine sir?" Killa asked with a humble bow and scrape as he filled the judge's glass. The important man replied with a wave of his hand since he was too important to actually speak to the help.

"I'm sure it's all just a coincidence. More black on white crime which proves we did the right thing," the judge assured them. He promised they would be home by Monday. That gave him a couple of days to fuck the trailer trash. In theory anyway.

Once all the glasses were filled Killa backed away to watch the show. A few impatient jurors took sips before the judge could stand to make a formal toast. He babbled some bullshit, they clinked glasses, sipped, and swallowed.

"What's the name of this wine?" juror 3 wondered and picked up a bottle. She first frowned at the odd name, and then the familiar face on the label. "Is this the boy?"

"It is the boy!" another shouted recognizing Randal Martin's face on the bottle. Not a smiling yearbook photo, but the autopsy photo complete with a hole in the head.

"Is this a joke?" the judge demanded looking directly at Killa. He was the only black man in the room, so it had to be his fault.

"Qisas," Killa explained the Arabic word on the label. "It's the law of equity. An eye for an eye."

By then, the toxic ingredients had done their job. All in attendance got dizzy and then died. Qisas.

****

Agent Bartow received the detail to guard defense attorney Daryl Queen as a punishment. He openly spoke up about the farce of a trial and paid for it. What better way to punish him than to make him guard one of the conspirators. Real funny indeed.

As head counsel for the notoriously racist K.A.N.A.S., Queen was very fond of the "N" word. Even his wife and 8-year-old son tossed the epithet around casually, as if the black agent didn't have ears. He heard the word so much it was like a bad rap CD.

"Finally!" Bartow sighed in relief when the unmarked car containing his relief pulled to a squeaking stop in front of the house. He glanced at his watch to see how late he was so he could get him back the next day. Qisas.

"Where's Brand?" Bartow asked the unfamiliar agent who approached the house.

"He got tied up. I'm Forrest," Killa offered along with his firm handshake. He wasn't lying either because the regular agent was actually tied up. He was in the trunk; tied up.

"Did you make out a 10-17?" the agent asked dubiously.

"But of course," Killa replied hoping it was the right answer so he wouldn't have to tie him up too.

It wasn't and that please the agent immensely. 10-17 was the code for a bowel movement so he knew what was to come. He probably would have murdered the family himself if he had to sit through one more round of nigger jokes over dinner.

"Have fun," Bartow said with a smile. He looked back at the future crime scene and left.

"How many niggers does it take to...oh, you're new," Queen said as Killa walked in. "Hope you don't mind nigger jokes. Freedom of speech and all that."

"I love a good nigger joke! Please, go on," he said truthfully. Seriously who doesn't love a good nigger joke?

"Tell him the one about how many niggers it takes to guard a family Dad! I love that one," the little racist child begged.

"I would love to hear that one," Killa urged as Mrs. Racist came in from the kitchen.

"Another one? Sheesh, doesn't the bureau employ whites? I'm sick of all these black men in my home!" Mrs. Queen fumed.

"I assure you, I's the last black man you have to deal with," Killa said politely. He even broke into a little tap dance to accompany the black Sambo voice.

"Ok, so anyway, Agent, how many niggers does it take to guard a family?" Queen chuckled heartily since he knew the punch line already.

"Um...one?" he asked taking a stab at it just for fun.

"None!" he screamed laughing hysterically. At least he died laughing when Killa sent a big slug right into his big mouth.

The kid ducked under the table and crawled to the other side. He stood up and tore out of the dining room. Killa let him reach the front door before shooting him in his little racist back. The boy slammed into the door then slid down. He went to join his dad where all racist of any race go.

"Wait, wait, wait!" Mrs. Queen shouted down the barrel of the gun with her hands raised in surrender. "I love niggers!"

"Huh?" Killa asked scratching his head with his gun as the soccer mom began to twerk.

"Turn up! Turn up!" she said then dropped it like it was hot and got her eagle on. She would have made her ass clap too if Killa hadn't clapped her ass.

"The prosecutor and man of the hour George Zeigler, you got next!"

Chapter 7

In breaking news, the judge and remaining jurors from the high profile George Zeigler trial were all found murdered in a downtown hotel. They had been sequestered once again for their safety after four other jurors were the victims of homicides. While authorities admit they are being targeted, they don't know by whom. Police currently have no leads... However, Islamic extremists have been blamed for this as well as everything else that goes on in our country.

"I know who did it," Yolo sang as she watched the news. She rubbed her growing belly proud of what was in it and who put it there. The baby inside seemed to respond by shifting and turning. Yolo watched the rest of the off the wall theories in amusement. Her boo wasn't the only one making news though. You know who else was back at it again.

****

It took the doctor weeks to heal after the fierce battle with the chief of police. To the victor goes the spoils and he got his head back. The chief lost his though. After Doc killed him, he separated them and put them in separate holes in the backyard.

Doc was a wise man and had stashed away a good sum of money during his loveless marriage. When he grew tired of Texas, he headed back to Atlanta. After he secured his stash, he copped a condo in a downtown high-rise. The plush digs afforded whoever could afford it a magnificent view of the city. Especially the nearby clubs and bars. Once again, it was time to hunt.

"Well hello pretty lady," Doc smiled at the pretty lady perched on the adjacent bar stool.

"Five hundred," she shot back looking him up and down to see if he had it.

A woman can gauge a man's net worth in a glance. Although that truth varies from white to black. Doc's tasteful slacks and loafers put him in the 50k or better bracket. The watch, tan, and two hundred dollar haircut doubled that. Easy for white people but niggas...

A nigga will wear two hundred dollar tennis shoes with four hundred dollar jeans and a hundred dollar t-shirt and still ride the bus. Thousands in jewels but be dead ass broke. Fifty-thousand dollar whip and live in an apartment complex. Spend hundreds 'turning up' every single weekend but gotta 'put something' on the light bill, or just enough to keep the phone on. Turn up!

"Cut to the chase huh? I like that!" Doc cheered. He knew premium whores charged a premium price and didn't mind paying it. Especially since, he was taking it back. They certainly wouldn't need it where they were going. "Let's go!"

"Let's," she agreed cheerfully and stepped down from her bar stool. The night was still young enough to turn a few more tricks. They walked out of the bar arm in arm like a real couple. "Head is extra you know," she said reading from her menu of sexual add ons. There wasn't much she wouldn't do as long as the price was right.

"I definitely want your head!" Doc gushed looking at her long slender neck. "I'm Doc, and you are?"

"Elaine," she replied truthfully.

She had never adopted a whore name like the other girls who worked the bar. Most of them were named after a jewel or a flavor. Diamond, Sapphire, Emerald, and Vanilla. She wasn't a whore; have her tell it. She just sold a little pussy. A little pussy and a lot of head. It seemed most customers wanted head. She hoped she wouldn't need a jaw replacement when she got older. No worries there because she wasn't going to get any older. Her last birthday was her last birthday.

"Nice!" Elaine exclaimed when they entered the condo. One thing about the Doc was he had good taste. The living room looked like a showroom dipped in leather and glass. The floor to ceiling windows exposed the whole city.

"Thanks," Doc grunted as he led her into his second favorite room. The room he had dubbed 'the playroom.' He liked his trophy room best.

"Huh?" she asked of the odd interior. The entire room was covered in thick plastic sheeting and a lone video camera sat mounted on a tripod. "What kind of freak are you? That's gonna cost extra!"

"I get a lot of squirters," Doc admitted as he slipped his ISIS type mask on. He turned on the camera and grabbed a sword.

"That's gonna cost extra too!" Elaine insisted of the long blade.

"Are you," he asked while taking a swipe that took her head clean off. It did a somersault before landing at her feet with a thud. The body stood there for a few seconds as if unsure what it should do. Finally, gravity got the best of it and down it went.

"I believe we discussed something about some head?" Doc asked Elaine's head as he picked it up. It didn't say yes, but it didn't say no either so Doc pulled down his zipper and got some head. With his nasty ass.

Once Doc finished he cleaned the head and prepped it for the trophy room. Inside the room was a glass display case. In it, were empty jars waiting to be filled and he intended to fill them all as soon as possible. Bonita of course had top honors on the top shelf.

****

"So how in the world are we supposed to get at them now?" Bigs griped as Killa drove behind the heavily guarded convoy. George Zeigler and the prosecutor were being shuttled to an undisclosed location for safe-keeping. It was now or never.

"Trust me, I got this," Killa replied handing him a black box with two buttons.

Big Shawn looked back and forth between the red and green buttons before deciding to press the green one.

"No!" Killa shouted just in time. "Not yet."

"What does it do? What are the buttons for?" he asked.

"A roadside bomb. The red button arms it and the green is to detonate," he replied filling the car with silence.

"Where in the hell did you get a roadside bomb? I'm an arms dealer and I can't get one!"

"I know a guy," Killa replied offhandedly.

"I need the hook-up. These shits would sell like hotcakes. Introduce me to the source!" Bigs demanded.

"Um...see what had happen was..."

"You killed him," Big Shawn finished, shaking his head.

"Had to yo. Dude was on some fake ass Jihad shit planning to blow up a mall or some shit. Trying to tell me that terrorism is a legitimate strategy of war in Islam. He a damn lie! Islam forbids terrorism. Even in war, you're not allowed to target non-combatants! Not allowed to destroy crops or livestock so how the fuck you gonna blow up the mall!" Killa espoused. "The mall? I love the mall, they got some good shit in there!"

"How you know so much about Islam?" he wondered.

"I know a guy. Ok, get ready...red button now."

Big Shawn pressed the red button causing a manhole cover to slide open as the vehicles approached. Inside there was a massive shape charge facing straight up.

"Wait for it, wait...for...it...now!" Killa shouted.

He pressed the green button just as the SUV holding the celebrity murderer and his accomplices ran over the manhole. The earth shook as the violent explosion shot up and into the truck blowing all of the occupants out of the windows and doors.

Zeigler flew out sideways and slammed into a building. The prosecutor shot fifty feet into the air before landing back on top of the flaming truck. That's as far up as his slimy ass was going in the afterlife. It was all downhill from there.

"Yo that was dope!" Bigs cheered. "Who's next?"

"I need to find that crazy bitch who killed my son," Killa growled.

"The one you got pregnant? I still don't see how...never mind. I got all my people on it and got nothing. That phone is routed through twice as many countries as yours is. We have to wait until she pops her head up.

"And when she does I'm going to cut it off. She'll turn up sooner or later," he guessed correctly.

"Speaking of turn up! Have you seen that interview by that dumb ass rapper Verb?" Big Shawn asked with a pained expression etched on his face.

"Nah, who dat?"

Chapter 8

I bare witness that there is no God but I
I'm the reason why I'm so fly
I'm the reason that time passes by
I am your Lord the most high!

"What the fuck?" Killa grimaced as he scrambled to turn the radio off. He was so flustered that he dropped the remote and was subjected to the perfidy for a few more seconds before he could turn it off.

The repugnant look on Big Shawn's face when he spoke of the rapper Verb caused Killa to look him up. He was not ready. The man was the lowest of the low. A complete piece of shit. Sometimes when moving one's bowels it gets pinched off, others break apart. Every now and then, you get a good spiral going like soft serve ice cream. A good coil if you will. A complete piece of shit. That was Verb.

The song was offensive enough but the more Killa looked, the worse it got. He came across a recent interview that made things go from bad to worse. Dude had sealed his fate and he ain't even know it.

It's ya boy da Verb. Dey call me Verb cuz I be about dat action. All I do is drank, smoke, fuck, dance, rap, and sang. Dem's all verbs! Oh and turn up! Dat's a verb too...

Verb was born Vernon Russell in a small Alabama town. His low IQ technically put him in the mentally retarded category but he was handsome and cool enough to attract followers. Somewhere along the line, people lost their identities and looked for something or someone to belong to. As long as they could scream out their clique, gang, posse, or squad they were happy. Technically that's called dick riding, but that's another story.

Dude was so influential that smart kids deliberately did poorly in school to be cool. Suddenly dumb was the new smart. Luckily, for him rap music had dumbed down enough for him to excel. His nursery rhymes were just catchy enough to catch on. First, he became a local celebrity then moved to the ATL. He blew up and soon the youth of the nation were hanging on his every word. And check out the stupid shit he had to say!

...I'm bigger than Martin Luther King! Who the fuck is he anyway? What he ever do? Could he sang? Did he rap? He ain't even have his own dance! Who name demself after a street anyway!

...Parents! Who da fuck is a parent to tell dey kid anything! Fuck a parent! Can dey sang? Do dey rap? You 'posed to turn up but dey tryna make you turn down...

...School? Fuck school! What a nigga ever learn in a damn school? I ain't never learnt shit in no school...

...Got bitches protesting a nigga fo' calling bitches, bitches! Fuck is' I 'posed to call a bitch? Only two kinda people in da world, niggas and bitches. Oh and bitch ass niggas so dats what... Fo'? No five!

...The bible? Huh? Dem just words. I write words, I can write a bible! Shoot I shoulda been in da bible. I'ma write my own bible. I'm God!

"Oh I gots to kill this blasphemous bastard!" Killa assured himself. That was the most sickening shit he had ever heard. To make matters worse, kids around the country were following the dude. He had to be put into the past tense for the future of society. A purge.

Killa began his mission to rid the planet of Verb by doing his homework. He followed, plotted, and planned to murder the man and not make him an icon. He just needed to disappear without a trace. He also discovered that he needed a vagina to get close to him.

With Sincerity in hiding, there was only one other female he could trust. Killa pulled out his trusty satellite phone and made a call.

****

"Mmm...right there baby. Right there!" Cameisha moaned as Trigga made circles around her swollen clit with his tongue.

He had become quite proficient at easting pussy from plenty of practice. She was on the verge of erupting when the satellite phone rang. For a split second, the earth stopped rotating.

"Shit!" She cursed mourning the loss of a good nut and sprang to her feet. Poor Trigga had a confused look on his wet face. She would have to explain later because family came first. A frown contorted her pretty face wondering if the call was good or bad news. The frown flipped upside down when she saw the initials U.K. on the screen. "Uncle Killa!" she cheered confusing her boyfriend even more.

"You ok? Your voice is trembling," Killa asked concerned about his niece. She might be a dangerous girl, but still a girl.

"Yes, I um...fine," she sang slightly embarrassed. Killa caught on and shook his head in amusement.

"Sorry to interrupt but I need some help."

"Say no more. When? Where?" Meisha shot back not caring about the who or the why. Anybody could get it. Anybody would get it when it came to family.

"A'ight. Meet me at the zoo in an hour," he said and disconnected the call.

"Ain't the zoo closed?" she wondered after glancing at the clock. She did a mental calculation before turning back to her man. "You got ten minutes, make them count."

Cameisha spread her thick thighs offering the pretty, plumpness that lived there. Trigga plunged in and went to work. Long firm strokes that echoed in the otherwise silent room. He picked up the pace when he felt her begin to shiver and shake beneath him. Cameisha came with a brutal grunt. Trigga was right behind her and bust a nut of his own. He collapsed on top of her but there was no time to cuddle. They had two minutes to spare when she rolled from under him.

Cameisha grabbed her cell and called her right hand woman before jumping in the shower. After rinsing the sex off she selected an outfit. She knew her uncle wasn't taking her ballroom dancing and dressed appropriately. Black jeans, black sneakers, black hoodie, and black gat.

"And where you going?" Trigga asked since he was her man and all.

"Family business!" she shot back and then softened since he was her man and all. "My uncle needs my help bae. I'll be back in a few, ok?"

"Sure shawty," Trigga replied. He knew he had as much control over her as she did over him and accepted it. He lifted his head to accept the kiss on the forehead she offered then watched her ass as she departed.

****

"There he go," Cameisha said seeing a flashlight flash on and off. She led her friend in that direction until they came upon a man holding the door open. The uniform he wore said he worked there and the tag on it said his name was Wali. "Thanks Wali," Meisha said politely as they stepped inside.

"In front of the lion's den," Wali replied pointing the way with his head. A smile decorated his face as he watched both girls' asses shift in the moonlight.

"Hey Unc!" Cameisha screamed when she saw Killa and ran to him. Ran into him actually, and embraced him.

"Hey niece," he replied with a grunt from the impact. During the hug, he looked past her at her friend and ran his eyes up and down her fine frame. "And who's your friend?"

"Oh that's my girl Jackie. Jack, Killa, Killa, Jackie," she formally introduced them.

The three killers meeting outside the cage were more dangerous than the killers inside the cage were.

"Hello Jackie, you got a man?" Killa asked shaking her hand while peering into the windows to her soul.

"No," Jackie giggled shyly ducking her head.

"Uh huh! Yes you do! Ralphie, remember?" Cameisha reminded her of the man she just left at home to come meet her.

"Oh yeah," Jackie laughed as she came back to her senses. Killa had that effect on women so he was wise to use it.

"Well if she's with you I know she's with you," he said trusting his niece's judgment. Lames hang with lames. Just as thorough people do. Birds of a feather and all that.

"No doubt! So who's going bye-bye?" Meisha asked. She was ready to knock whoever off so she could go get back in bed with her man.

"You ever heard of this rapper called Verb?" he asked.

"I have! Dude is a fucking dumb ass! Son got a damn cult following. Got kids dropping out of school, using drugs, and disrespecting their parents!" Jackie shouted in disgust.

"You mean that dude with all the writing on his face? The one who said he's the new God? Please let me murk this nigga," Meisha growled causing the lions to stir as if they understood. All they picked up on was the violence.

"You no, me yes. I need you to lure him to me. I need to kill him," Killa said almost somberly.

Cameisha felt him and didn't push the issue. "Ok Unc. No problem," she said matching his tone.

"You want me to wait with him while you go get him?" Jackie offered looking the handsome murderer up and down.

"Girl no!" Cameisha laughed. "Besides two asses are better bait than one. You can help me get the nigga."

"I don't mind you know," Killa teased his niece as they departed.

"Bye Unc!"

****

Getting next to the rapper proved to be easier said than done. For one thing, the dunce had a long line of groupies eager to donate their vaginas to his cause. That was despite his well-known aversion to condoms. He was an advocate of unsafe sex and deadbeat parenthood. His anthem to his 12 known baby mamas entitled "Not My Problem," was a hit.

They dressed sexy the first time they tried to get next to the rapper and got nowhere close. Not with the half-naked sluts hovering around. One girl had cut holes in her shirt so her nipples came out. Turn up!

Jackie and Cameisha had to swallow their pride and dress sufficiently slutty to get noticed. They had to meet at the house to change since neither of their men would have allowed them out of the house like that. They suited up in matching Daisy Dukes and sheer half shirts. Both of their nipples peered through the fabric like an extra set of eyes. It was uncomfortable on so many levels, but it worked.

"Who y'all bitches?" Verb demanded when he spotted them in the club. Cameisha actually flinched from the abrasive word but luckily, Jackie had her arm.

"I'm Jackie and dis my gi...bitch Cameisha," Jackie said trying to keep a straight face. She contained her laughter into a brilliant white smile against her lovely black skin.

"Jack!" Meisha exclaimed through clenched teeth at her using their real names.

"Ain't like he gon' live to tell anyone," she said plainly right in front of him. She knew that he was a dumb ass that wouldn't catch on. He was an inanimate object like a lamp or houseplant. She owned shoes smarter than him.

"I'm tryna fuck!" Verb announced like an official proclamation. It was his signature line and always worked. That time too.

"Okay!" Cameisha and Jackie sang like groupies.

"Let's ride!" he said and stood. When he stood, his two bodyguards did too. Meisha twisted her lips ruefully, hoping they had life insurance. Hoping they had told their loved ones they loved them recently since they wouldn't see them again.

"They comin' too?" Jackie pouted in an effort to spare the men.

"Dey gotta go errwhere I go. Dey ain't gon' see us all fuck dough," Verb said being the gentleman that he was. "My condo is big!"

"We stay not too far from here. We can do it there, that way y'all don't got to drop us off," Meisha suggested.

"That's a good idea boss," one of the two guards said. They readily agreed since it would be them doing the late night drop off after the rapper had his way with them. A task they had dubbed 'taking out the trash.'

"It would be best," the other one co-signed. The rapper had far too much company in his home to keep him safe. He made their job that much harder with his reckless lifestyle. "Safer than bringing more people to your residence."

"Ok," Verb agreed mainly because he didn't know what the word residence meant. He didn't want to ask in front of the girls. Didn't want to seem dumb you know.

"Here?" the driver frowned unsure if he had heard correctly.

"Yes, here," Cameisha reiterated pointing to a rundown tenement building. The guard pulled up and they all got out.

As soon as the two guards stepped their four feet on the sidewalk, they dropped dead. Verb looked confused as usual but Killa stepped from the shadows to explain. The smoke billowing from the tip of the silencer said what needed to be said.

Verb lifted his chin proudly ready to accept what he thought was a robbery, like a man.

"Ugh!" Killa grunted as he socked the rapper with everything he had. The punch knocked him down and out, but the brass knuckles broke his jaw on both sides. He wouldn't be saying any more dumb shit that night. Or ever, for that matter. Killa dragged him into the backseat and jumped behind the wheel. He tossed his niece a set of keys and pulled off.

"Hey!" Cameisha wailed as he sailed away. "Man!"

She accepted the fact that she was going to miss the main event and hit a button on the key. A car across the street beeped and flashed its lights in reply.

"Guess that's us," Jackie sighed in defeat.

"Let's go. I gotta change before I go home. Trigga will lose his mind if he sees me like this."

"That's exactly why I ain't changing," Jackie said wickedly.

****

Verb was snoring loudly from the punch, drugs, alcohol, and lack of sleep. Killa poured the rest of his soda on the man to wake him up once they arrived at the zoo.

"Get up and get out!" he demanded.

The confused man tried to speak but his broken jaw wouldn't allow it. Instead, he grimace and moaned from the pain. "Qrst!" was all he could manage through his shattered face. It was some more dumb shit but luckily, Killa couldn't make it out.

As soon as they got inside, Killa sent a silent slug into his ass cheek. "No!" he shouted in pain. He looked at Killa and asked why with his eyes.

"You got a ten second head start. I catch you and I kill you," he replied.

Verb took advantage of the head start and took off running. He had no idea of where he was or where he was going so he darted his eyes in every direction as he ran.

"Quick, in here," Wali suggested holding a door open for him. "Trust me; he won't follow you in there!"

"Hijk," Verb nodded in thanks and rushed inside.

Wali closed and locked the door behind him and went around joining Killa. "It's show time!" Wali announced and hit the lights.

The lions were already sniffing the air for the smell of fresh blood. When the lights came on, and they saw that fresh meat and they smiled in thanks. Verb wasn't smiling though. He couldn't believe his eyes so he blinked and rubbed them. It didn't work though; the lions were still there.

Female lions are usually the hunters. They make the kill to feed their family. They began a slow creep towards the creep until the male lion let out a low growl. It obviously meant, "Y'all fall back," in lion talk because that's exactly what the females did. This one was his.

"Efg! Hijk, hijk!" Verb screamed at his dilemma. It was the first and last time he ever got his alphabet correct.

"Just tell them who you are!" Killa yelled with a chuckle.

"Or turn up!" Wali cracked up getting in on the fun.

To Verb's credit, he did put up a fight when the lion pounced. He threw a nice jab but the lion ate it. It snatched his arm completely off then moved in for the kill. Once the lion crushed his neck, the girls moved in. Killa captured the meal on his phone for his own amusement.

"Well that was fun!" Wali cheered once the show was over.

"It was," Killa smiled briefly then became morbid. His thoughts turned to 'who's next?'

Chapter 9

"I wanna kill you, you P.W.T, we gonna kill you, you P.W.T," Tikisha, the local mean girl screamed an inch from Jane's ear.

Jane wasn't hard of hearing or anything; Tikisha was just a fucking bully. The song she sang was a twisted spin on the Michelle Jackson song "P.Y.T." Instead of pretty young thing, P.W.T. stood for poor white trash. Jane was white and poor but far from trash. Her luck was just bad. Actually, there's no such thing as luck, good or bad just decree.

What had been written for her was a messy divorce between her parents. Her wealthy father said fuck them after he fucked his young secretary. He traded his old wife and old life for a new chick with new tits. Since he could afford a good lawyer and she couldn't, he ended up with it all while she got nothing.

Jane's mom took a job and did the best she could do. Her meager earnings forced her to move into the hood of Atlanta's southwest side. She quickly found out that some blacks are just as racist as some whites can be.

Jane was the lone white student in the whole tenth grade as well as the only one on the school bus. She would have walked to and from school if it weren't a ten-mile trek. Instead, she was subjected to Tikisha and the abuse. Not a day went by that she wasn't verbally abused. Not to mention getting beat up or jumped on a couple of times a week. It was becoming unbearable for the lonely young girl.

"You should just kill yo'self bitch!" Tikisha suggested so close to her ear she could feel the heat from her breath.

It actually sounded like a good idea at that moment. Her mother couldn't help and the teachers nor the principal would help her. Jane was nearing the end of her rope in more ways than one.

"Die bitch die!" Tikisha demanded marching behind her to her apartment. A vicious slap to the back of her head served as a goodbye as she entered.

Jane stared at the stranger in the mirror and shook her head. She didn't even recognize herself. Her pretty golden locks had been snatched from her scalp. Tikisha had removable hair and couldn't live with Jane having real hair. Her blue eyes were black and blue from numerous beatings.

She glanced around the sparse apartment and reflected back on the huge suburban home she'd left behind. The run down complex had more empty crack sacks than blades of grass. Even her college fund had been looted for designer purses and custom breasts for Daddy's new wife.

"She's right you know. You might as well kill yourself," Jane told her vague reflection. The imposter shrugged as if she didn't care one way or the other. That settled it. She took a deep breath and exhaled a sigh. "I'll do it then."

Jane marched straight into her bedroom and into the closet. She looped one end of her belt over the bar and the other around her neck. A lone tear fell at what could have been as she sat down. The drop wasn't far enough to break her neck as in a classic hanging. No, she slowly strangled herself to death.

She could have simply stood up and lived, but that meant more Tikisha. She shook her head no at that thought and pressed on. A few seconds after that she blacked out, and a few seconds after that she was gone.

****

"My daughter killed herself because she was being bullied! Bullied, beat up, and made fun of for months! We reported it. We told the principal and the teachers. We did everything that we were supposed to do," Jane's mother Dianne wailed in a heartbreaking interview. She had just put her only child in the ground and contemplated joining her. Her reason to live had just been buried.

"That girl is pure evil! Why won't someone do something? Why won't someone help before she kills someone else's child?"

The nationally televised interview was felt by millions. Everyone was sad and angry but one viewer more than most. One who recently lost a child of his own. One who hated racists and bullies with his whole heart. Still, he might have left well enough alone if not for the next interview.

"My baby ain't did nothin' to dat gurl!" Boquisha spat with Tikisha standing defiantly by her side. The mother and daughter were only 15 years apart and looked like sisters. Both cute under all the ghetto girl accessories and busting out of their matching ghetto girl outfits. "Dat bitch was weak and kilt herself."

"Shole did," Tikisha chimed in along with her mother.

"Fuck dat bitch and her mama and anybody who don't like it!" Boquisha proclaimed in her native Ebonics. Multiple childbirths had interrupted her childhood so she just continued acting like a child well into adulthood. She smoked, drank, and turned up along with her children.

In the current climate of instant celebrity where losers can become famous for being famous, the two ratchet girls were set to be stars. They formed a mother-daughter twerk team with gigs booked all over the city. Their video had gone viral already. They even signed a three-book deal with Bitch Book Publishing and were set to be best sellers.

"Show 'em how we do it!" Boquisha demanded. "Turn up!"

Tikisha responded automatically as if a button was pressed on her turn up remote. She closed her eyes, raised her hands, and shook her ample ass. Momma joined her and they went into one of their routines. They were stars in the making, but...along came a Killa.

****

Killa walked into the club and stopped just short of thrusting his fingers into his ears to escape the assault on his eardrums and soul. Some dumb ass rapper said nigga so many times he shot a glance to the DJ booth to see if the man spinning was wearing a hooded robe. The song "Kill all Dem Niggas" was rapped by a black guy but actually a K.K.K favorite. They played it at all of their functions as well.

The DJ flawlessly mixed the next song "Fuck Dese Bitches" and the crowd went wild. Killa stifled a laugh thinking about the late Verb. He didn't say fuck dese lions when they were eating his ass.

He looked to the stage and saw who and what he came for. There were Boquisha and daughter Tikisha twerking on the stage. At least twerk rhymed with work because it was a close as they ever came. Oh and were they working! The mother-daughter twerk team bent at the waist and popped their asses in unison. Big brown ass cheeks protruded from matching boy shorts in perfection. Killa looked back and forth between the two and got an erection somewhere along the line.

"May as well," Killa said as the thought of fucking them both before killing them crossed his mind. Halfway through, that same thought disgusted him and he shook it away. It was a good thing Antoinette sashayed into his life when she did.

"Excuse me," she giggled after intentionally bumping into him. Not hard enough to make him spill his drink, but enough to distract him from the hoochie mama and daughter on stage. Killa was hot at the bump and ready to add the bumper to the night's death toll. Until he turned and saw her that is.

"Watch where the fu...oh my," Killa gushed when he locked eyes with the brown stallion. She was just his type standing 5'11" in her wedges with her natural hair pulled into a wavy bun. Oh and thick, he liked thick. "I mean I'm sorry for bumping you."

"It was I who bumped you and I meant to do it," she admitted getting caught up in the brown gems he called eyes. She batted her own eyes before extending a hand. "Antoinette."

"I'm Killa," he answered accepting the dainty hand while shooting a glance back at the stage.

"Somehow I can't see you being interested in them?" she asked scrunching her face as if 'them' had an odor.

"Purely clinical, but you, you could get it," he assured.

"Get what?" she asked seductively, but the glance she shot down to his crotch rendered the question rhetorical.

"My number," he blurted as the show came to an end. He quickly quoted the number to one of his phones and rushed to catch up to his victims.

There was a long line of freaks who wanted props for bedding the wenches together. Bragging rights for fucking the mother and daughter at the same damn time. They offered cash while Killa offered stars. Or to at least make them stars.

"I would like to shoot the both of you," he offered behind a smile at his clever word play. He would like to shoot them but that was too quick, too easy. They were not getting off that easy.

"Both of us together?" Boquisha asked with dollar signs in her eyes. They had fucked the same men separately but never together. "That's gon' cost extra!"

"Shole is," Tikisha agreed. She had starred in many a fuck tape but this would be her first time being paid for one.

"How about I pay both of you enough money to last the rest of your lives?" he asked.

Boquisha and Tikisha snatched Killa out of the club so fast he almost got whiplash. He directed them to his car and made the short drive to a hotel where he rented a room. Of course, it was under a fake name so he couldn't be charged for cleaning up the mess. And it was going to be messier than a ratchet girl's time line.

"This is nice," the women sang at the four star digs. Most of the rooms they had been in were motels or motor lodges. Or the back seats of cars.

"It gets better, strip!" he ordered digging into his bag of tricks searching for treats for the tricks.

The females wasted no time in complying. They peeled off the damp boy shorts filling the room with not so freshness. The musk of underarms combined with the salty odor of overused vagina wafted towards the ceiling. Heat rises you know.

"What the..." Tikisha protested when she saw the pistol.

"Shh..." Killa whispered holding the long silencer up to his lips instead of an index finger. It meant the same thing so they muted themselves.

"Well come on," Bonquisha sighed and dropped to her knees and opened her mouth. It wouldn't be her first blowjob at gunpoint.

"Uh no" Killa laughed and pulled the next items from the bag. "I'm sure you guys heard about the ice bucket challenge?"

"Uh huh, yeah we have," they both agreed eagerly.

"Well, this is the ice pick challenge," he explained.

"What we 'posed to do with these?" Tikisha inquired.

"Kill yourselves. Winner gets to live a little while longer," he said crossing his fingers behind his back. His ass was lying. The winner was getting shot in her head.

"I ain't finna..." was all Boquisha got out before her daughter attacked. Tikisha snatched a handful of weave and stuck her mother right in her neck.

"Bitch!" her mama yelled as she came out of her weave. She thrust a blow into her daughter's cheek.

"Fuck," Killa giggled as he scrambled to start the recording. It was supposed to be for Dianne but he decided to keep a copy for himself.

Both ghetto chicks were good fighters and it was an all out brawl. Not only did they poke and gauge with the ice picks, but punched, clawed, and kicked. Blood skeeted to the ceiling during the fierce battle. Once they were both weakened from battle and blood loss they gave up on defense. They just took turns stabbing each other. They dropped to their knees still stabbing. Finally, they landed one last jab in each other's necks and keeled over dead. Killa took their pulses ready to shoot whoever had one.

"Good job ladies," he giggled leaving the dead women in the room.

****

As soon as Killa stepped from the hotel, his phone began to vibrate on his hip. He smiled broadly knowing exactly who was calling. It was new pussy, and that's something to smile about.

"Hello," he answered in his sexy voice instead of the killer voice.

"Killa? What a name, this is Antoinette. I just called to see if you wanted to...um..."

"Fuck your brains out? I would love to!" he said pressing the issue. Had she said no he would have gone to bed.

"Sure!" she sang and gave him directions to her vagina.

Antoinette kept a nice, clean little apartment in midtown. When Killa arrived, she opened the door and posed in her sheer nightshirt. The light from the TV behind showed off her thickness. Since it was already established that they were fucking she took his hand and led him to the bedroom. She climbed on her bed and watched as her guest stripped down to his birthday suit.

And what a birthday suit it was. Killa obviously had been doing some sit-ups and push-ups because his pecs and abs were perfect. The caramel colored birthday suit came fully equipped with a thick erection pointing straight ahead. Antoinette was so pleased she actually clapped.

"You wanna see my trick?" she asked spreading her legs as Killa climbed on the bed.

"Sure," he eagerly agreed as she began playing with herself. Pussy is good and new pussy even better but a pussy that does tricks is priceless. Bet they won't make a commercial out of that.

He watched as the vagina swelled, glistened, and bloomed. A line of juice escaped then ran down. Suddenly, a jet of fluid shot out and hit his leg startling him.

"What the fuck was that?" he demanded as he scooted away in fear.

"I squirted!" she giggled quite pleased with herself.

"You peed!" Killa shot back looking at the pee on his leg.

"Un uh, I'm a squirter!" Antoinette insisted with a nod.

"Do it again," he said backing out of pee range. She complied and made more lovely little circles on her pretty pink button. A few seconds later, it happened again.

"Uh uh! See!" he answered seeing it clearly came from her urethra. He knew enough about vaginas to pull the wool over his eyes. "It is pee!"

"It is," she admitted lowering her head in shame and came clean. Well, almost since she did just pee. "It happened by accident once cuz I had to pee real bad. The guy I was with went crazy and told me to do it again so I did. Been peeing on dudes ever since."

"Just nasty," he chided and got off the bed. He looked around and found the bathroom and went in. He had worked up a good lather when Antoinette came in.

"Can I join you? I peed the bed," she said sheepishly. Killa responded by moving forward so she could enter. She took the washcloth and said, "Let me."

Killa grunted and allowed her to wash his body. After gently cleaning him, she used the soapy cloth to tug on his dick. Once it was erect once more, she rinsed it and knelt down. He closed his eyes and leaned back enjoying the feel of her hot mouth. It got even hotter when he filled it with pent up frustration. To her delight, he stayed hard.

Killa led her back to the bed and bent her over. They couldn't get back in cuz it had pee on it. As soon as he rolled a condom on, he slid inside of her. He delivered firm back shots that echoed in the room. Antoinette's knees buckled when she came causing her to collapse on the bed. Not the pee part, so Killa went with her and kept on stroking. After Killa bust a nut of his own, they ended up back in the shower.

After getting clean, dry, and dressed, Killa hit the door. Before he departed, he left a last word of advice. "Stop peeing on people!"

Chapter 10

As the age old adage goes, everyone will have his or her fifteen minutes of fame. Greg Williams was an exception and got his times three. You first heard of him when he starred in the public service announcement entitled 'The Lady Killer.'

In it, he detailed a year of his womanizing antics. He had unprotected sex with scores of women and at least one man. It culminated in him receiving some bad news. Or did he? That would be the million-dollar question.

His second fifteen minutes of fame came when he was arrested a year later for having reckless, unprotected sex after being diagnosed with HIV. He had infected fifty women and at least one man. The trial was national news and everyone was watching. Everyone.

The case was the proverbial open and shut, slam-dunk. The fifty victims at twenty years each meant a one thousand year sentence. The State of Georgia would leave his ass in there for a thousand years too. He would be eligible for parole in 750 years. In the end, it all came down to his testimony. The prosecutor couldn't wait to get the crass, arrogant man on the stand.

"Did you have sex, unprotected sex, with all the women in the complaint?" he asked dramatically flailing the sheet of paper as he spoke. He handed it to the defendant who looked it over before speaking.

"Can't really say, I don't remember most of them hoes names," Greg shrugged and handed it back. "I fucked all them," he announced smugly as he pointed to the twenty victims in attendance.

The jury let out a collective gasp at the admission of guilt as well as the disrespect. It was going well until the prosecutor fucked up. He opened his mouth real wide and stuck his big ass foot right inside. It was support for the old saying "quit while you're ahead."

"So after being formally notified that you were HIV positive you continued having unprotected sex with women and...and him!"

"Actually I was never formally notified of nothing. Shit for all I know one of them bitches gave that shit to me! Or him," Greg shot back causing the victims to gasp that time.

"Order! Order in the court," the judge demanded to quell the murmurs. He was on their side but had to keep control of his courtroom. He wanted no errors that could be overturned on appeal.

"Oh no?" the prosecutor chuckled and produced his proof. "I submit exhibit 9-A. The transcript of the "Lady Killer" public service announcement!"

A hush fell over the courtroom as he leafed to the last page. He licked his thumb dramatically, cleared his throat, and began to read. "...'What kinda doctor is you anyway? Askin' 'bout who I fuck?' The doctor, a state employee replied 'State law requires us to notify all sexual partners of new HIV infections' end quote."

"Ok and? He ain't say I had it did he?" Greg asked causing his lawyer to spring to his feet. He thought the case was lost so he pounced on this information.

"Objection! State protocol was not followed Your Honor! There is a standard script for notifications and record does not reflect that it was followed!" he cheered.

"Both sides approach!" the judge boomed down in frustration. The prosecutor and defense attorney met him at his throne for a heated yet muted debate.

"You better not!" Killa growled as he watched the proceedings live on his TV.

"It's clear Your Honor, he was never formally notified. Not per state requirements," the defense attorney argued.

"Um, I um..." was all the prosecutor could come up with. He knew he was right, the doctor fucked up.

"Fuck," the judge grunted loud enough to be heard across the courtroom. He frowned at what was to come and dismissed the lawyers to go stand by their tables. When he opened his mouth to speak, the whole country listened.

"Due to the fact that the state protocol for HIV notification was not followed...the case is dismissed," he croaked painfully.

The courtroom went wild. Not only did the victims in the pews wail and moan but the jury as well. Greg fueled the fire by triumphantly pumping his fist.

"Order in the court!" the judge demanded, banging his gavel. That did nothing to calm the grieving so he cleared the court.

Once the jury and spectators were cleared Greg was free to go infect more unsuspecting women and at least one man. Would have too, except along came a Killa.

****

Gregory laid low for a week or so after the trail. The whole business had taken a toll on him as well. He hung around his apartment for the most part, only venturing out for the occasional errand. Every time he left his house, he had the feeling he was being followed. That's because he was, death was right on his ass. When he finally decided he needed some pussy death followed him to the club.

As usual, Greg scanned the crowded club for the baddest chick in the building. That's how a real player starts and works his way down. The rest would get his number to be hit at a later date. A good club night can eventually net ten to twenty new kills. Literally in his case since he was The Lady Killer.

No fisherman throws his hook in the water alone hoping to catch a fish. You need bait. Killa was a good fisherman and he had some great bait.

"Hey handsome," Antoinette sang seductively as she mounted the bar stool next to the fish. She and Killa had linked up on a regular since she stopped peeing on people.

Greg looked the pretty brown thing over and regulated her to his hit list. "Hey yourself pretty lady," he replied showing his pretty white teeth and green eyes. He had his eyes on a pretty red bone he wanted to infect but this one could definitely get it down the line. The sick bastard came to the conclusion that since the virus was given to him; he might as well pass it along.

And pass it along he did. Besides, the known fifty victims there were fifty more who still didn't know they were sick. That hundred infected became two hundred and that two hundred infected two hundred more. Talk about a social network!

"Can we go somewhere and chill?" she asked running her moist tongue over her full lips as a question mark. It was sign language for 'I give good head.' She had no idea why Killa wanted to lure the man out and didn't care. He had been laying the pipe so well she would do anything he asked.

"I wish I could but I have something to do," he said meaning the red bone. "Shoot me a number and I'll hit you later, from the back."

"Mmm, that's how I like it! Only I don't have a phone," she offered sadly, poking her lip out. Suddenly a bright idea popped up and cheered her up. "Why don't you just come by whenever you finish doing whatever you have to do? I'll suck your dick."

"That's what's up!" he eagerly agreed just as she knew he would. That's a nightcap most men wouldn't pass up. He beamed brightly as she scribbled her address on a slip of paper.

Antoinette handed him the paper and stepped down from the stool. They exchanged smiles before she turned to walk away. Greg watched her ample ass shift from side to side, as she left. Had he looked up he might have seen her wink at Killa on the way out. Her mission was complete so she headed home to wait on her late night plumber's visit. Killa would be coming to lay some pipe.

Killa watched Greg approach the pretty, light-skinned girl he had set his sights on. They smiled, chatted, laughed, and then stood up. He didn't know what it was, but Greg's game was A-1. Five minutes after meeting her, he was leading her off to slaughter, literally. Knowing he couldn't allow him to leave with her, he had to think fast. Time for some good old fashion cockblocking.

"Gregory Williams, I'm Xavier Forrest from...Black Ink Magazine," Killa announced holding his cell phone out as if recording. "How do you feel about being acquitted of fifty counts of aggravated assault?"

"Aggravated assault?" the pretty girl gushed. She liked bad boys but had no idea how bad the boy really was. She was about to find out though.

"That's right. He infected fifty women and at least one man with HIV. Didn't you see the trial?" Killa asked wondering how she missed the media circus.

"Was it on the video channel?" she asked explaining why she knew nothing of world events. If she couldn't twerk to it, it didn't concern her. Turn up.

"HIV!" she squawked, pulling her hand from his. She grimaced at her own hand hoping she hadn't caught it and took off to the bathroom.

"See that's some real bullshit right there!" Greg lamented coming face to face with his executioner. Another step and Killa would have beat him to death on the spot. He was relieved when he didn't because he had something else in store for him.

"Lucky for you, I got another bitch on standby nigga! Or else I'd beat that ass," Greg announced plainly.

"Sho you right, I'll see you later," Killa laughed as he marched out. Killa pulled up his phone and got Wali on the line. "Get everything ready. It's almost show time!"

****

"Cock blocking ass! I should've whoop that nigga's ass," Greg muttered to himself as he drove to the address Antoinette gave him. He pulled up to the house and double-checked the address on the paper. The house looked abandoned and dark, but still, the promise of good head spurred him on. When he tapped on the unlocked door, it swung open.

"Hello?" Greg called as he stuck his head into the house. Suddenly the lights came on then went back out when Killa caught him with a vicious punch with his brass knuckles. That was bad enough, but when the lights came back on...

"What the fuck? Where am I? Where are my clothes? Ouch!" he rambled when he awoke. He shielded his eyes from the blaring light with one hand and gingerly touched his swollen face with the other.

"Not sure about the fuck. The where is a lion's den and your clothes are the least of your concerns," Killa said through the zoo's P.A. system. On cue, Wali cut the spotlight so Greg could see. And oh to what he saw.

The first thing he noticed is that he was inside a real lion's den. He grew up in Atlanta and had been going to the zoo his entire life. Luckily, there were no lions in sight. The next thing he noticed was twenty of his victims on the spectator side of the glass. Nineteen women and one man.

"Fuck y'all bitches want? Some more of this?" he taunted grabbing his infected dick and wagging at them. Yep, it was real funny, at the moment anyway.

"Showtime ladies and um...gentleman," Killa announced.

The audience replied by hitting the record function on their smartphones and pointing them. Greg was about to say more slick shit until a door slid open and the lions sauntered in. Neither the lions nor Greg could believe their eyes. The dinner was just as surprised as the diners were.

"Help!" Greg screamed shrilly as the bitch in him came out. In his defense, he was about to be eaten.

The male lion sat, cocked his head, and watched as if amused. The spectators were clearly amused. They jumped at the chance to watch the man who changed their lives die. Some would never marry or bare children because of him and his dirty dick. Sure, they played a role in it and they would have to live with that bad decision.

Greg fought the good fight. First, he tried to climb out but kept slipping back down. If the expert climbing lion couldn't climb out, he certainly couldn't. Next, he tried to get through the glass. He pounded, kicked, and begged but got nowhere fast.

The male lion stood and inched forward as his women flanked their prey. They were only there to cut off any escape; this was his kill. The lion pounced and grabbed Greg by this throat. The bite sent a spray of blood into the air as it nearly severed his head. The victims captured every bite as the pride moved in and devoured the man.

"Thanks for coming out, God bless you, good night," Killa announced through the speakers once the show had concluded. That marked the end of his chapter, and this one.

Chapter 11

Doc was a pretty sick dude and as a result, he did some pretty sick shit. I guess that's bound to happen if you sit around talking to heads all day. Sooner or later, the heads start to talk back. It wasn't unusual for Doc to pull out a head or two for a date. That night was one such night when he had a double date.

Of course, he brought out Bonita, his favorite. She sat at the head of the table while Janelle flanked her left. The black girl was his latest addition and arrived by luck. Good luck for him, but for her, not so much.

Doc had been out on the town head hunting and struck completely out. No one went for his pick-up lines so he went home alone. As he drove along a skinny, crack-stitute flagged him down. She was hardly his type, but curiosity killed the cat. He pulled over to see what she wanted.

"You want some head?" she offered generously.

"Do I! I want some head very much," he shot back and hit the automatic locks. Doc had just received a package from China and couldn't wait to try it out. He hoped it worked as well as they claimed. You wouldn't believe what you can buy online these days.

"Oh this is ni..."

"Yeah, yeah, nice, I know," Doc muttered impatiently as they entered the condo. He practically dragged the woman down the hall to his playroom. "Stand right...here."

The crack head watched curiously as the doctor donned his mask and tore into the package. He came over, slipped it over her head, and read the directions. Janelle figured whatever was going on was worth another ten bucks. Her normal routine was suck, swallow, and smoke. This was extra.

"Shush!" Doc fussed when she began to speak, distracting him from the directions. One side of the sheet was written in Mandarin and the other in broken English. "Ok, position...hit switch...fuck!"

The BD 2000 was the bootleg version of the D.C. 2000 but worked just about as well. A little slower and not as smooth, but got the job done nonetheless. The crack head's crack head popped off and fell at her feet. Crack heads are as tough as Tonka trucks so the frail body just stood there. It fell a minute later when Doc picked up the head.

"I do believe we spoke about some head?" he asked holding Janelle at eye level. Fresh heads are the best heads to get head from so he wasted no time. With his nasty ass. Once he finished he put her in a jar and added her to his collection. Her body was placed back in the same alley where he got her. It was found the next day.

Doc often cooked for the girls on date night but they never ate. Formal dates like that required wigs and make-up while Doc rocked a tux. The girls were great listeners and loved to hear his stories about his infamous former patient.

"So I told Killa that I...wait a second...what's going on here? I see the way you guys are looking at each other," Doc announced. Never mind that he positioned them that way. Doc tossed back the rest of his wine and scooped the girls up. He whisked them into the living room so they could all get cozy.

"Hey Bonita," Janelle said in her ghetto girl fashion. She would have moved her head like a ghetto girl too if she had a neck.

"Hola mamacita," Bonita giggled. The girls bantered back and forth flirtatiously until Doc leaned them in for a kiss. He got rock hard, well pebble hard, watching them kiss.

"Can I get in on the action?" Doc asked.

Neither objected so he sat Janelle down and whipped out the wood. You couldn't tell ol' Doc nothing as he got head from the two heads. They even fought playfully over him at times. Doc was a good referee and let them share. Once he finished he let them share that as well. He then cleaned them up and put them back in their jars. With his nasty ass.

"Good night ladies," Doc sang to the six women staring back at him. Yup, six and it was about to be a problem.

****

"In breaking news the headless body found last week was positively identified as that of Janelle Morris age 25. She brings the number of headless women to five in just over a month's time. Islamic extremist are being blamed for the attacks..."

"Islamic extremist!" Doc screamed after spitting his coffee across the table. "What the fuck is an Islamic extremist?"

He was always amused and bewildered by the oxymoron favored by the media. Islam means peace and submission so an Islamic extremist would be someone who is extremely peaceful. He also wondered why the faith of other people who commit atrocities was never mentioned. It also made him wonder if news and media agencies had a hatred for Islam and Muslims.

"Those are my kills! Mine! Mine! Mine!" he raged at the reporter on the screen. She of course could not hear him so she continued lying on Muslims.

Doc was livid. He hated living in the shadows while everyone heard of Killa. He vowed again to kill him as soon as he found him. Luckily, he knew enough about the man to know where to find him. If not him, at least his grandmother.

Chapter 12

"Man!" Killa groaned when Jay-Z began rapping from his cell phone. Only one person had that particular ring tone assigned so he already knew who it was. Still, he checked the satellite phone first to make sure he didn't miss a call. He didn't, so he answered. "Hello, Grandma."

"Hello yourself, I need you to stop by the store for me please," Diedra requested just like she would any other time. Only this wasn't any other time and she was supposed to be in hiding with Sincerity and the kids.

"I'm not even in New York, why are you?" he asked shaking his head. "Why are you home? You're supposed to be upstate!"

"Chile I got tired of being cooped up in that place. I'm an old lady and I want to be in my own place," she insisted.

"I'm on my way," he said and clicked off. His next call was to his childhood friend Nitty to provide security for his family until he arrived.

"A girl? You worried about a girl?" Nitty asked in utter astonishment. After all, he did grow up with him and knew his murderous reputation better than most.

"She's not a girl, she's a monster! If you see her, kill her! No questions asked, murder her!" Killa insisted.

"Say no more," his friend said accepting the responsibility. He put a team on the rooftops and one in the courtyard. It was not a good day to visit University Homes. Shit, no day really is, but that day less than others.

Killa had no time to drive the thirteen hours to New York so he headed to the airport. That was dangerous on so many levels, but mainly because he couldn't carry a gun. He felt butt naked without one. Same feeling one has when accidently leaving their cell phone at home.

Antoinette's offer of one for the road rang in his ears the entire flight. Turning down a girl who swallows is a tough pill to swallow.

Knowing Sincerity would be waiting with open arms and open legs gave him strength.

He couldn't help but shake his head and laugh at his plight. He had some wonderful women in his life, but they were both hardheaded. Why are the best women so hardheaded?

After an uneventful flight, Killa caught a taxi to the Bronx. He rode up the hill on Ogden Avenue and got out on 166th Street to walk the block over to the projects. To the casual observer he seemed to walk casually although his eyes darted side to side, up, down, and all around for possible threats. It was caution, not fear, even though they look alike. A commotion at the daycare center caught his attention. He wanted so badly to mind his business but couldn't. Not when a child was involved. Killa loves the kids.

"Girl shut your damn mouth!" the kidnapper demanded as she drug the hesitant child away from the center.

"No! You ain't my mother!" the child yelled trying to pull her hand free.

"Fuck," Killa groaned, knowing he couldn't just ignore a child being kidnapped. He figured he'd go rescue her and return her to the daycare. "Aye, what'cu doing with the kid?" he demanded as he approached the woman and child.

"Minding my damn business," she shot back. Killa couldn't help but frown at how odd she looked up close. The nearly bald woman had no eyebrows or lashes. Her bright skin had spots and blotches as if burned by chemicals. She actually looked like a lab rat. No telling what she might do to a child.

"Do you know her sweetheart?" Killa asked bending down next to the girl.

"No!" the frightened child yelled tugging her hand free. Just as the girl ran towards Killa, the woman spoke, stopping her dead in her tracks.

"Ladonquanishontayia! You know good and well I'm your damn mother!" she insisted with a stomp of her cheap sneaker.

"Mommy?" the child scrunched her face and asked upon hearing her hard to pronounce name. She was almost three and still couldn't say it.

"Yeah, it's me," she softened as her child came near. She turned to Killa to explain the mix up. "She ain't never seen me without my weave, make up, eyebrows drawn on, eyelashes, and contacts."

Killa just walked off shaking his head.

****

"Not my fault," Sincerity announced holding her hands up in surrender.

Since Nitty had shot him a thumbs up he went home first. "I already know once that hard headed old lady makes up her mind there's no stopping her," Killa conceded as he scooped his son up from the sofa. "Where's Rico?"

"Sleep. He sleepy too so..." she said leaving the rest in the air. The movement in the tiny shorts said the rest as she walked away. Both kids asleep at the same time meant one thing. Somebody was getting fucked!

"Rock-a-bye, go to sleep," Killa sang and rocked, rocked and sang. The child blinked and yawned like he was trying to fight it but the sandman whisked him away. The father gently laid him down and tiptoed away to get laid himself.

"He's slee...oh my!" Killa exclaimed when he reached the bedroom. There was Sincerity, butt naked, face down, ass up on the middle of the bed. Her plump vagina poked out the back like a ripe juicy mango. Guys like mangos.

Killa dropped his jeans and boxers as he made his way to the bed. By the time he got there, he was as naked as she was. The best thing about a mango is the juice, so he leaned in for a taste.

"Ssss..." Sincerity hissed when his tongue touched her juice box. He got reacquainted with it by kissing and licking it until she came in his face. He couldn't complain as many times as he done it to her.

Instead, he stood and used the gush of fluid to ease his way inside. He stifled a growl as he sank slowly to the bottom. The best part of the vagina is the bottom, sucks if a guy can't reach it. He's missing out, so is she come to think about it.

Killa slowly withdrew up to the head then sank back inside. He kept up that slow stroke until Sincerity squealed and came all over his dick. The sound and sight of all that creamy goodness on his dick pushed him over the edge. Kicked him off the cliff is more like it when he came with a grunt. At the last possible second he pulled out and skeeted potential children onto the tattoo on her back. That is what they're for after all.

"Boy you know I'm on the pill. Wouldn't want you to have two chicks knocked up at the same time," she quipped as she climbed out of bed.

Killa let the sarcastic remark pass without comment. What was there to say anyway? He stood by his decision to come clean about Yolo being pregnant. It was what is was and they had to deal with it. She had worked up a good lather when Killa joined her in the shower.

"You going to see Grandma Diedra?" She asked as she turned to wash her man. Starting with his dick of course.

"I guess I better. I got Nitty and them watching her."

"I put lil' Chris and the rest of those little goons in her hallway. Them lil' niggas work for weed," Sincerity replied.

Killa knew them little niggas were in trouble if Yolo did come. Nitty, the young thugs, were all in trouble.

****

"You hungry?" Diedra asked nonchalantly. As if she hadn't disobeyed his order and put herself in grave danger from the lovely little lunatic. She did cook his favorite foods hoping that it would help. It did.

"Yes," he sang like a six year old as the aroma of fried chicken, collard greens, candy yams, and macaroni and cheese invaded his being. The next thing he knew, his mouth was full of food. That shut him up.

"I know you're upset but I can't stay cooped up in that place. You need to do something about that woman so we can live in peace," she huffed.

"Mm hmm," Killa grunted because his mouth was stuck shut from all the cheese. Once he got it down, he put his foot down. "If I can't, you guys are going to South America. I bought enough land there for the entire clan."

"I'm not leaving my granddaughter!" Diedra insisted.

"Grandma that girl will be down there sooner or later herself," he replied knowingly. The Dope Girl was about to go to war herself and he knew it. Beef like that only ends one of two ways. A graveyard or on the run. Even jail isn't an option at that point.

Chapter 13

"So what's been up?" Nitty asked nosily as he passed Killa a blunt. He guarded Grandma without question but now he had a million of them.

"Nothing," Killa replied answering all of them at once. He took the blunt but stopped just short of taking a pull and passed it back. Too much was at stake, he had to stay sharp. "I see business is brisk."

"You would think so," Nitty said at his observation of all the drug activity. Killa knew all the young runners were running for him. "Fuckin' crooked ass cops don't want a nigga to eat!"

"Crooked cops! Where?" he asked eagerly. He still felt a need to purge and who better to rid society of than crooked cops! If there's one thing the world could do without, it's crooked cops.

"Detectives O'Neil and Garnett. Real pieces of shit!" Nitty grumbled. The look on his face was as if the names tasted like shit in his mouth when he spoke them.

"Same ones who killed that little gangbanger?" he asked remembering recent news reports.

"Gangbanger! Ha, son was a choir boy!"

William Clayton was actually a choirboy, a straight A student, and all around good kid. He made the fatal mistake of going to the store wearing a hoodie. Everyone knows black boys in hoodies are armed and dangerous. O'Neil and Garnett pulled up on him to search him, but Garnett panicked and killed him.

Instead of owning up to their mistake, they planted a gun on the kid. The orange hoodie wasn't the color of any known gangs, so they made one up. By the time, they dragged his name through the mud he was a gangbanging, gun toting bad guy. Oh, and an Islamic extremist for good measure.

Kevin O'Neil was indeed a piece of shit. Joining the police force gave him a gun, a badge, and permission to do whatever the fuck he wanted to. He was a degenerate gambler, drug addict, alcoholic with a blowjob fetish. A typical day for him started with a line of coke, shot of liquor, and a few tokes of weed before his morning piss. Then he would force his dick down the throat of one of the local prostitutes. They could either blow him or make bond. Then he set off around the Bronx shaking down and robbing criminals. He got so bad the criminals called the cops.

Dave Garnett was assigned to internal affairs. When the complaints reached his department, they put him on the crooked cop. Dave was supposed to be undercover and report back, but got corrupted himself. His mortgage, bills, and college for three kids made the easy money easy to take. He had very little field experience and shot little William by accident. He gladly went along with the cover up and they were free to resume their illegal activities. Would have gotten away with it forever, but...along came a Killa.

****

"You know this moke?" O'Neil grunted at the new face in the project's courtyard.

"Must be new," Garnett guessed after squinting didn't help identify him. "I never seen this one before."

"New nigga equals new money! Let's go introduce ourselves," O'Neil suggested and got out of their unmarked car.

"Sup my nigga?" O'Neil asked with a broad smile. That term never ceased to amuse him. Niggers used it as a term of endearment but to him it meant he owned your black ass.

"Say word?" Killa responded with a chuckle. He already planned on killing dude but he was going to eat those words before he left for the afterlife. "Sup with you?"

"These are our projects is what's up," Garnett shot back trying to sound tough and failing miserably.

"Yeah, we own it!" O'Neil jumped in. "You gotta pay if you wanna stay!"

"Shit I just bought this spot from Nitty. No wonder it was so cheap!" Killa lamented. He loved getting to try out his acting chops and was actually quite convincing.

"Guess he didn't tell you about the tax. A grand a day but that's cheap considering," O'Neil explained.

Killa nodded thoughtfully, even scratched his chin as he contemplated. Actually, he knew first-hand how much those projects could generate. Put out a collection box to feed the hungry and their asses were going to starve, but sell crack? The place was a gold mine. A grand a day was a bargain but Killa had a better offer.

"I don't have a problem with that, but check it...What about twenty racks up front for the whole month?"

The perfidious partners conferred with a quick glance and nodded their approval. Splitting twenty thousand sure beat coming up in the projects every day. Besides, they could and probably would renege. Who could he tell?

"Deal, let's have it," Garnett greedily demanded and thrust his empty palm out. It came back just as empty.

"Son, I ain't got it in my sock! I'll drop it off later, shit; I'll come to your house and deliver!" Killa offered hoping it would be that easy. It wouldn't be.

"We can meet you tonight, by the stadium. I'm not coming in this rat hole at night," O'Neil spat.

"I got a thing tonight, with the family," Garnett begged off.

"I'll meet him and uh...just bring your share tomorrow?" he offered.

Killa spoke and understood double talk and heard what wasn't said. His partner wasn't getting shit. O'Neil would kill Killa and keep the twenty grand himself. It warmed Killa's cold heart to be able to rid the planet of the scumbag.

"Ok, sure, thanks," Garnett said appreciatively. His naïve ass had no idea how much his so-called partner beat him out of.

"Well ok," Killa agreed half-heartedly. He would have loved to get them both at the same time.

"My nigga," O'Neil chuckled as they walked off.

****

"And where are you headed?" Sincerity asked seeing Killa dressed to kill. Not suit and tie dressed to kill but boots and jeans dressed to kill. All black murder gear.

"Gotta go holla at some cop friends of mine," he replied as he accessorized. Not tie pin and cuff links, but Kevlar and extra clips. That night was one of those nights that had people in mourning by morning.

"Sucks for them," she laughed knowingly. "Want me to stay up?"

"I do, I do," he shot back just as knowingly. Murder always got his adrenaline going and she wanted to feel it. The couple met lips like couples do and he was off into the night.

Since Killa didn't have a definite plan, he planned to be amorphous. Instead of driving or taking a taxi, he walked the short walk down the hill to Yankee Stadium. A game was in full swing, which could work for or against him. Plenty of people to mix with, but also plenty of potential witnesses.

Killa wasn't the only one with murder on his mind. Detective O'Neil had mentally spent that twenty grand twenty different ways. He planned to buy a shit load of drugs and pussy. He would kill him and make up an excuse for his partner. He was so busy plotting and planning he didn't see Killa approach from the rear.

"Sup," Killa said instead of shooting him. He wanted to, but too many people were near.

"My nigga, you got my money?" O'Neil asked trying to conceal his shock. The thug had the drop on him and could have dropped him. The fact that he didn't, gave him a false sense of security. Rocked him to sleep.

"Yup, in my car," he replied, pointing up Jerome Avenue with his head. The cop looked down the dark block and smiled.

Killa lead the way waiting for the right second to strike. They both discreetly pulled silencer equipped pistols out as they talked about what might be happening in the stadium behind them. The roar of the crowd could be heard blocks away, which was good for a Yankees fan. Bad for crooked cops though.

"Right there," Killa said pointing at a sedan on the curb.

"The blue one?" O'Neil asked in disbelief. He couldn't be talking about his car, could he? He was.

"Yup," came the reply that started the gunfight. Both men pulled their guns and fired. Both went stumbling as slugs slammed against bulletproof vests. Both sought refuge behind the cop's car.

"Shoulda known you had a vest on," the cop complained in pain. Vest or no vest, getting shot hurts.

"I knew you did," Killa laughed. "That's why I used cop killers."

"Cop...killers?" O'Neil grunted and put his hand up to his vest. He had taken a round to the vest before and it hurt, but not like he hurt at that moment. The blood on his fingers explained the burning sensation in his chest and shortness of breath. He was dying and he knew it. The best he could do now was take his killer with him.

He used his last bit of energy to jump up and attack As soon as he stood; Killa put one of the Teflon coated bullets into his forehead. His brain flew out of the huge hole in the back of his head like confetti.

"My nigga," Killa chuckled as he looked down at the mess.

He dug into his pockets pulling out weed, coke, and money until he found what he was looking for. His phone had more intel on his partner than he would have thought. Not just phone number and address, but pictures of wife, kids, and parents. It was more than he needed to continue his purge.

Chapter 14

Detective Garnett didn't buy the official report of his partner's murder for a second. Street robbers prey on visitors to Yankee Stadium on a regular basis, but they didn't use Teflon coated bullets. The specially designed bullets were designed for one thing, killing cops. Hence their name, Cop Killers.

It was a hit. That much he was sure of, but nothing more. They crossed and double-crossed so many people it would be impossible to figure out who. He was naïve enough to believe it ended with his partner. Besides, he had his own demons to deal with. He had a tail as he visited different cathedrals and churches seeking penance.

Killa could have killed him quite a few times over the few weeks he followed him but found his depression amusing. Dude was clearly going through it and he loved it. Loved watching his guilt eat him alive. He started drinking the day his wife took the kids to her mother. The time was finally ripe for his demise.

Knowing his routine allowed Killa to get a step ahead of him. Just like a spider, he spun a web and waited. As soon as Garnett got caught in the trap, along came a Killa.

"Bless me father for I have sinned," the cop stated as he crossed himself.

"In what way?" the substitute pastor asked through the partition.

"You name it. I've broken every trust, betrayed every covenant. My job, my family, my oaths. I've lied, cheated, stolen, even...killed," he said contritely.

"Killed? Who did you kill son?" Killa asked holding the gun to the partition. On a whim, he pulled his phone to record the confession. Little William's family might enjoy it.

"I'm a cop. Detective David Garnett," he announced with both pride and shame audible in his voice. "I um...killed a man, a boy, actually. It was an accident. My partner said the kid was a drug runner. We were going to take his money to buy lunch. We did that a lot, rob people. Most of our days were spent robbing or extorting people. Hell, we went weeks on end without making an arrest. Just pay your bail on the spot and go on about your business."

"Who was the boy? Tell me about the boy you killed," he urged. He already knew, but wanted it on tape.

"His name was William Clayton. It was all over the news a few months back. Good kid, a freaking choirboy. I mean the kid actually sang in a choir! We made a monster out of him. Really soiled his image. Planted drugs in his pocket, a gun in his hand. Lied about run ins we had with him. His family knew it was some bullshit but...excuse me..."

"That's fine son. It is some bullshit. Please continue."

"What's my penance Father? I'll do anything. Charity, fasting, um...anything! Just tell me what to do!"

"Kill yourself," Killa suggested after stopping the recording. He aimed his gun through the partition again just in case he refused.

"Really? That's not to say I haven't thought about it. My piece has been in my mouth twice this week."

"Do it. Do it now. Put your weapon in your mouth and pull the trigger," he urged as his own finger tightened on his trigger. Either way, dude was dying.

The cop's service weapon sounded like an explosion as it went off in the small space. Killa rushed out of the stall and into the next. There was the cop staring off at whatever dead people stare at. The top of his head was open like a sunroof. Blood and brain matter dripped from the ceiling.

"My nigga."

****

Killa caught the train back to the Bronx with back shots on his mind. It was all good until a kid plopped down beside him and started talking non-stop.

"As salaamu alaykum!" the bright-eyed teen greeted.

When Killa grunted a reply, he launched into his spiel. Killa stared out the window as the child rambled on with the enthusiasm of the newly indoctrinated. He was content to let him ramble until either of their stops came until something caught his attention.

"Say that again!" Killa snapped his head and demanded.

"It's every Muslim's duty to do Jihad! We must kill all infidels!" he repeated just as he had been taught. It was then that Killa noticed he was just a child. His features made him look twelve instead of his sixteen years.

"Who told you that?" he asked turning his lips like 'yeah right' at the false teaching. The teacher would have gotten beat up if present.

"My shake!" the kid said proudly. "Cut off their heads!"

"Don't you mean sheikh?" he corrected even though it had to be a shake and not a sheikh to feed him that mumbo jumbo. No real religious scholar would teach that to a kid.

"Oh yeah, sheikh," the kid corrected with a giggle. Killa's son's face flashed in his vision for a second.

"I need to speak to this sheikh of yours," Killa insisted. "Where is your masjid?"

"We don't have one. We meet at the sheikh's apartment," he said and gave the address. "This is my stop."

Killa returned the kid's greeting and repeated the address to commit it to memory. The kid grunted as he heaved his heavy backpack onto his back. He couldn't help but wonder what was in it. He didn't have to wonder for long. Just as the train pulled away from the platform, the kid smiled, waved, and blew up.

****

The massive blast totally erased the child and those closest to him. The shrapnel in the bomb spread out and claimed even more lives. The explosion rocked the departing train and knocked it off track. When it ground to a halt, Killa pried open a door and made his escape.

Since he was no stranger to the underground labyrinth that was the subway, he easily maneuvered away. He used a service exit and climbed to the street above. Killa was far too traumatized to raise his hand to summon a taxi so he set out on foot. He crossed over to the Bronx on the 159th Street Bridge and hoofed it up the hill. Luckily, there were no Yolos or Docs around because he was in a daze. He didn't even recognize his buzzing phone to answer it.

"Are you ok?" Sincerity shouted when Killa walked into the apartment. She ran over and slammed into him so hard the hug ended up in the hallway.

"Uh...yeah, I think so," he replied unsurely. He had seen and caused plenty of deaths and destruction during his stay on the planet but what he'd just seen fucked him up.

"They said a train blew up and I knew you were on that line. I been calling and calling and..."

"Yo, I was right there. I seen that shit yo!" he said still amazed by it.

"What kind of monster would do that? All of those people," Sincerity moaned as they made their way back inside.

"He was a kid. I was just talking to him and..." Killa frowned as the scene replayed in his head. He recalled clearly seeing both of the boy's hands. "He didn't set it off! He was murdered too!"

Chapter 15

The second deadliest terror attack in the city claimed over a hundred lives. In any other city, it would have topped the list but 9/11 was a tough act to follow. The boy and those closest to him were evaporated by the powerful blast. Thousands of pieces of shrapnel consisting of nuts, bolts, screws, and nails spread out claiming more lives. Of the survivors in area hospitals, several more were not expected to live. Some had limbs knocked off, none would ever be the same.

Video of the attack was captured from eight different angles from eight different cameras. It took no time to put a name to the face of the bomber. In fact, it was his own mother who made the report. She couldn't believe her son was responsible even after watching it over and over on every channel.

Derrick Johnson or DJ as his single mother Jennah affectionately called him was by all accounts a good kid. An impressionable young boy looking for a father figure like most fatherless boys. Most of the boys sought refuge and tutelage from the drug dealers but not DJ. He was tricked by a charlatan Imam.

The so-called sheikh Shajji was a complete sham. He was really a disgruntled former Army sergeant named William Dent. A complete fuck up who failed at everything he ever tried. Of course, that was the government's fault. He still insisted that whitey was holding him back even though the president was black and his own mother was white.

He was too black to join one of the white supremacy anti-government movements, and too light for any of the militant black groups. Like most Americans bombarded with anti-Muslim lies and propaganda he assumed the local Muslims would support his cause. The thought wrong because the majority of American Muslims are just that, American Muslims. Islam is their way of life and America is where they live. He was warned about attempting to spread his nonsense around the Muslims until they finally made him stay away.

That's when Sheikh Shajji decided to make his own sect. They were called the Islamic Revolution and were about as far away from Islam as could be. There was no prayer, no charity, no belief, and he wrote his own bible. The kid was right; he was a shake.

Shajji's congregation consisted of local teens who came over to smoke weed and watch terrorist propaganda videos. No one really believed him except young DJ. That's how he ended up with a backpack full of explosives without knowing it.

****

The FBI, DEA, ATF, CIA, NSA, and BET were all on the case. When you have that many alphabets on your ass, it usually means trouble. Usually, but not always. In this case, the security agencies focused on Islamic groups, masjids, and schools. They got absolutely nowhere. Killa had something they didn't have, an address.

"823 Boston Road," Killa repeated aloud as he had been for days since the bombing. The shock of the incident initially wiped it from his memory, but media references to the Boston Marathon bombing brought it back.

He repeated it again as he stood in front of a tenement building bearing those same numbers. This was the where. Now he had to find the who. Killa stood there scrutinizing every face that came and went. He had just dismissed a forty something black man when he came out and lit a cigarette. Sheikhs don't smoke menthols. Plus the man was clean-shaven and dressed like the teens dressed.

"Sup Sheikh!" a youth called out in passing getting a salute in return. He had found the who, now came the how. Killa mentally debated on whether he should shoot him, stab him, choke him, or use the DC 2000...

"Sup yo?" Sheikh Shajji asked when he noticed Killa staring at him. Good thing he couldn't read minds because Killa's was full of murder.

"What's up is the damn country, this damn president, congress..." he whined like anti-government types often do. It was bait and the sheikh bit.

"I know, right!" he agreed and launched into one of his blame filled tirades. Everything was everyone else's fault. Killa nodded in agreement with every lie and complaint. The sheikh had a new recruit.

It took a few weeks of listening to his babble before being invited upstairs. As soon as they walked in, he knew he had his man. He saw several backpacks that matched the one carried by DJ. A table containing various components caught his eye. The casual observer would have dismissed it as clutter. Killa wasn't the casual observer; he was a bomb expert himself.

"What you know about that?" Shajji asked seeing his guest eyeing the hardware.

"Nothing, but I'm ready to learn," Killa replied with wide eager eyes.

"It's simple really. C-4 and or black powder, nuts, bolts, screws, and nails from the hardware store for shrapnel. The detonator is then attached to a cell phone. That way, I can set it off from here. Make the call, and instead of hello, it's good bye."

"Mmm," Killa grunted and held his composure. It was proof that the kid wasn't a suicide bomber. He was a victim too. The shake was about to be a victim too.

It took another week of blunts and videos before Killa was ready to make his move. The blunts were cool, but the videos were trash. A bunch of lies. In all the time he spent with the so-called Islamic extremist, the man never prayed once. Everyone knows Muslims have to pray five times a day but Shajji never did. All he did was smoke weed, drink beer, and eat ham and cheese sandwiches.

"I'm ready. I want to be a martyr!" Killa announced triumphantly at the end of an Al-Qaeda video.

"Prove it!" Shajji dared. "There's a big peace rally downtown to-morrow, take a pack."

"I'll do it," he accepted. To prove it he rushed over and grabbed one of several identical backpacks from the table.

The two men armed the device inside in total silence. When the shake went to relieve his bladder Killa made some adjustments of his own. The stage was set; it was show time.

Shajji was going to miss the only adult company he had with Killa gone. At least the neighborhood teens would hang out to smoke weed with him. He watched the coverage of the peaceful rally waiting to see Killa. When he spotted the backpack, a sinister smile spread across his face. He made a big production of pressing each number and hitting the send button, but nothing happened.

"Huh?" he asked when he saw Killa on screen answer the phone. "Hello?"

"Not hello, good bye." Killa laughed as the timer ran out of time.

The shake tried to say something else, but the bomb turned him in-to confetti.

"Who can I kill next?" Killa pondered aloud as he walked away. Luckily, for him, there were plenty of people in need of killing.

Chapter 16

"Chop...chop...chop...chop," Sincerity's vagina sang with each deep slow stroke of Killa's thick dick.

Her moans and whimpers sang back to her splashing box. His deep growl provided the bass to the sexual symphony. A fucking concert.

"It's talking to you daddy," she purred and arched her back.

"Mmm," he replied listening to it squish and squelch beneath him. It was the elusive great pussy. 90% of all pussy is good, but great pussy is rare.

Killa looked down and was treated to a private porno show as he watched himself slide in and out of his woman. A puddle of special sauce had accumulated at the base of his dick and begun to drip to the bed below. He felt her shiver, shake, and explode from yet another orgasm. Killa wasn't far behind her.

Truth be told, every time he fucked his girl doggy style, Yolo came to mind. The lovely little lunatic had some great pussy too and he couldn't deny it. Not to mention it was brand new. He recalled pushing past her hymen into the comfortably cramped space. Every time he thought about it, the same thing happened...

"Argh!" he grunted and released deep inside his woman. Any deeper and she would have had cum in her lungs. She could have drowned. He fought not to scream as she massaged his manhood with her strong vaginal muscles. Killa lost that battle and woke the baby.

"Your turn," Sincerity giggled and rolled out of the bed. Killa was too out of breath to complain and she got away. He got some get back by wiping the sex off him with her nightshirt. After pulling his pajama pants on, he scooped up his son.

Sincerity returned from the shower with a smug smirk on her face. It was real funny until she pulled her shirt over her head and felt the wetness.

"I swear I hate you!" she growled and giggled. "Just nasty! Watch your back homie."

"Homie?" Killa laughed.

He realized how fortunate he was to have her in his life. A satisfied smile spread on his face as he watched her surf the web. Probably going on social media to brag about getting her boots knocked properly.

"Ew! Nasty bastard," she spat as she opened her inbox and saw a dick pic.

"Let me find out you a wood watcher!" he laughed.

"This nasty ass nigga keep flirting with me. I told him I was twelve and he sends me this! Child molesting ass…"

"Child molester?" Killa asked excitedly. He was ready to purge once more and who better to brutally murder than a child molester!

****

Thirty-year-old Adam Gulliam was a perverted child molester. Have him tell it, he just like them young. Real young and that was real sick. He deserved every bit of what was coming into his life. That fact that he invited it made it all the better.

He made a fortune online and used it to rent little ghetto girls. There were plenty of young girls in his upscale Long Island town, but that was too risky. People cared about those kids. No, the little ghetto kids were safer, easier. A lot of times, he could swoop in, pick one up, take her home, exploit her, and get her home before her mother finished turning up.

You would be surprised how many children are unsupervised online while Mama sips her malt liquor and arranges her spades hand. Songs and videos had made etceteras so important that a lot of girls sold themselves to get them.

Sincerity had posted a sixth grade picture of herself on her profile to keep the wolves at bay. It had worked for the most part, but that was how Adam liked them. The rabbit teeth and pigtails turned him the fuck on.

When he contacted her, she replied that she was twelve and his response to that was a dick pic. A fresh erection from the goofy picture she posted. He would have gotten blocked had Killa not been present. Instead, he was going to be killed.

"That's going to cost you," Killa warned in reply. "I'm her dad."

"How much? I'll pay," he shot back instantly. His own father was a sick freak too so he didn't bat an eye.

"Tell him those new sneakers everybody is wearing," Sincerity suggested. Being a mother made her take interest in his murder.

Adam agreed to buy the child for the price of the sneakers.

"I wanna watch," Sincerity pouted while watching Killa get dressed to kill.

"As soon as I get back," he replied with a wicked grin. He misunderstood thinking she meant watch when he went down on her. Honest mistake since he always wanted to watch when she did him.

"No, I wanna watch you kill him. I wanna see it!"

"Just see?" Killa prodded to see if she wanted more. She did.

"No, I want to do it. I want to kill him. What if that wasn't an old picture of me? He sent that picture of his dick to who he though was a kid," she spat murderously. It's in everyone; it just has to be brought out.

"Get dressed. I'll drop the kids at Grandma's," he replied. He saw the look in her eyes and would not deny her. "How sweet, my baby wants to purge."

****

"You need gas baby," Sincerity advised along with the low gas light. Just then, the alert began to beep cosigning her.

"Huh?" Killa asked. He sounded irritated at being snatched away from his thoughts. She pointed at the gas light rather than disturb him further. "Oh...yeah."

Killa pulled into the first gas station he saw and the first thing he saw was four young black guys. The thugs looked out of place in the upper middle class neighborhood. It immediately pissed him off because kids like that gave all black people a black eye.

Jeans slung low off their asses, unlaced sneakers, and boots. One had a gun on his t-shirt; two had weed plants, while the last one's shirt proudly proclaimed 'Fuck the World.'

He was pretty sure that wasn't the dream Martin Luther King dreamt. The goons were probably waiting on some white people to victimize. Had Killa not had more pressing issues, he would have pressed the issue.

"Need anything bae?" Sincerity asked as he began to pump the gas.

He grunted and shook his head no, but she was going to get him something anyways. His eyes zeroed in on her swaying hips as she walked into the store. He wasn't the only one. The goons all figuratively pulled out shovels and began to dig their own graves.

"Sup ma, you fuckin' or nah?" 'Fuck the World' wanted to know. He grabbed his crotch just in case she didn't understand. His jeans were so baggy all he had was cloth, but it didn't matter because he was still getting killed for it.

"Can't speak bitch?" Weed Plant One demanded when Sincerity turned her nose up at them and kept walking.

Weed Plant Two added that she must be a lesbian, stuck up, etc... None of it was true, but again it didn't matter, they were all dying for it.

Sincerity was steaming mad when she had to walk back through the soul train line of insults and disrespect. It only got worse when she got back to the car. "You think that shit is funny!" she barked at Killa who was cracking up. He did think that shit was funny, but they were all going to die anyway.

"I'm saying though, you are stuck up. Probably a lesbian," he laughed and teased until they reached their destination.

"You have arrived at your destination," the GPS announced royally as they pulled into the driveway.

"He could get a woman if he wanted!" Sincerity said as she looked at the nice house and manicured lawn. "This dude is sick."

"Was," Killa said ready to go put him into the past tense.

As he walked towards the house, the light along the walkway lit up towards the house. Right before he reached the heavy oak door, it swung open.

"Is that her? Bring her up!" Adam demanded as he burst from the house. He was so eager to get a child he looked through Killa.

"I gotta check the place out first," Killa advised as he slipped his brass knuckles on.

"Ok, ok! This is the foyer, that's..." was a far as he got before getting knocked out cold. Killa waved his woman in and dragged their host into his living room.

"Damn! Who was he 'posed to be, Michael Jackson?" she frowned seeing the kiddie play land the child molester had set up.

"Give me the zip ties," Killa instructed as he sat Adam up in a chair. She complied and he secured his wrists and ankles.

"Oww...oww..." Adam moaned as he awoke from his nap. "Why? Who...what's going on here?"

"You sent a picture of your dick to a twelve year old and you're going to die for it," Killa explained.

"Huh? Wait! I sent a picture of my dick to a lot of young girls and nobody killed me! You're taking this too far!" he reasoned.

"You're not helping yourself, you know that right?" Killa laughed.

"Wait, wait, what is that?" Adam demanded as Sincerity slipped the DC 2000 over his head.

"The Decapitator 2000, it's really cool!" Killa cheered.

"Don't hurt me, please...I'm sick. I need help. I'm a victim too," he pleaded getting a brief stay in his execution.

"What's that mean?" Killa wanted to know.

"I was molested too. My uncle, he made me...do stuff. I never told anyone but it made me like this," Adam sobbed.

"I read that a lot of abused kids go on to become abusers," Sincerity stated correctly.

"So you wanna give him a pass?" Killa asked unbelievably.

"No silly. Let's kill him too," she shot back.

"Makes sense?" he asked Adam who nodded in agreement. "Let's call him over."

Killa used Adam's phone and dialed as he dictated. When the man answered, he put it on speaker and held it to his face.

"Hey Uncle Jack, it's me Adam," he began.

"Adam?" Jack asked wondering what made his nephew call him. They hadn't spoken since he got big enough to say no to his sexual advances.

"Yeah...um...remember when I was little and you used to make me suck your dick"

"What? No! That's a lie; that never happened! I..."

"I want to do it again," Adam jumped in cutting off the lies and denials. A brief silence filled the room.

"...I'm on my way!" Jack shouted and hung up.

"He lives about an hour away. You guys hungry?" Adam offered.

They declined and waited on Uncle Jack. Uncle Jack did twice the speed limit and arrived in half the normal time.

"I knew you liked it...what are you?" Jack said dick in hand as Killa pulled the door open.

Killa ignored the question and pulled him inside at gunpoint. Uncle Jack saw his nephew as he looked around and nodded.

"Nice set up," he said admiring the child molester station. That got him knocked out too. When he awoke, he was in the same position as his nephew.

"See what you got us into," Adam chuckled dryly.

"What?" Jack asked, not quite understanding what was happening.

"They're going to kill us," he explained.

"Kill? Us? Why?" Jack moaned.

"Because you molested me and turned me into a child molester too!"

"I did no such thing!" he shot back like it was true. The men argued back and forth with Killa and Sincerity watching like a tennis match.

"Actually, you're going to kill him and she's going to kill you," Killa corrected. He took the device from Adam's neck and put it on his uncle's. Once he unzipped and freed his hand, he told him to hit the switch.

"Damn!" Sincerity and Adam both shouted when the head hit the floor and rolled under the chair. It took some doing to get Adam's wrist cuffed again. A right hook from the brass knuckles finally did the trick.

"Ok, ok," he muttered in defeat as the device went back over his head.

"You sure you up for this?" Killa asked giving her a chance to back out. She responded by hitting the switch and taking his head off.

"Man that was fun! Can I do another?" Sincerity cheered. Killa could only shake his head and laugh.

"Please Bae, please!"

****

"Where you going bae?" Sincerity asked when Killa disobeyed the fussy GPS's direction to turn right.

"To see if your little buddies are still at the store."

"Yay!" she clapped happily, causing him to shake his head again.

Sure enough, the same young punks were at the same place at the gas station. How foolish can you be to disrespect someone and stay put? That was about to cost them. Just as he pulled in, they stepped around back to smoke more weed.

"Wait here," Killa insisted and parked. He crept around the other side of the building to send the kids to the other side of life. He drew his pistol and inched forward using their banter as cover.

"So I told that bitch to beat it," Weed Plant One told Fuck the World.

"Bitches be buggin'," Gun Shirt proclaimed, shaking his head as if that explained everything. Like he just said some real profound shit.

"That's why I just fuck them bitches, and then say fuck them bitches!" Weed Plant Two shot just as Killa raised the pistol to shoot him. Luckily, his phone rang and bought him a few seconds. It's rude to shoot people while they're on the phone and everyone knows that.

"Shh! It's my mom!" Weed Two said urgently causing a confused frown to spread on Killa's face.

The kid's ghetto accent had vanished. He sounded just like a white kid suddenly. Amazingly, his disrespectful friends respectfully muted themselves.

"Hello Mother."

"The fuck," Killa whispered to himself as the truth came to light.

The kids were no thugs; they were imposters. The nerds were actually supposed to be at a sleepover at Gun Shirt's house. Like a lot of good kids, they wanted to be bad boys. All that rap music had fucked up their minds. There was no ghetto or projects around so playing dress up and standing in front of the store were as close to the hood as they could get. It almost cost them their lives that time. Almost, because Killa decided to spare them. Still, he was going to teach them a lesson they wouldn't forget.

"That was close!" Weed Plant Two sighed once he finished lying to his mom.

"My mom would totally freak if she found out we're out here," Gun Shirt seconded.

"Mine too. My dad said if he finds one more Verb CD in the house I'm grounded!" Weed Shirt One complained.

"Whatever happened to Verb?" Fuck the World wondered. They didn't get to ponder on the mystery much because along came Killa.

"What set y'all fools claim!" he demanded from behind the huge gun. The barrel of the .45 looked like a train tunnel up close. Fuck the World accidently peed his pants.

"We're not a gang!" Gun Shirt screamed as they all raised their arms high. So high, they were all on their tippy toes.

"Which one of y'all kilt Mook-Mook? You? You? You?" he asked pointing the gun in their faces. He fought back laughter as he stomped his   foot   with   every   word. "Which...one...of...y'all...kilt...Mook...Mook?"

"We don't even know any Mook-Mook!" Weed Shirt One pleaded. "We're not even in a gang!"

"I'm captain of the chess team," Fuck the World cried real tears.

"We're in the glee club," Weed Shirt One and Two sang together.

"I'm on the debate team," Gun Shirt added hopefully.

"So why y'all wearing all black? Why y'all dressed like thugs? Calling women bitches?" Killa demanded.

"It's the rap music sir. It messed us up," Fuck the World said still in tears.

"Ok, here's what we're going to do. First, get out them gang colors," Killa demanded and they immediately complied. "Put your drawers back on Fuck the World! Now, take your asses home! And no more rap music!"

"You are so childish," Sincerity cracked up when he returned to the car. She could still see the near naked boys running down the street behind them.

Later in life gun shirt went on to become a senator. Weed plant one and two both lawyers. Fuck the world became a doctor and tried to save the world. He did the kids a real favor. Luckily some real thugs didn't come along and harm them. The police can't tell the difference between bad kids and good kids playing dress up. They were on the path to destruction but luckily....along came a Killa.

Chapter 17

In breaking news, two headless men were discovered in a Long Island home. Adam Gulliam and his uncle Jack Wilcox were murdered while tied to chairs. Police found a large cache of child pornography and accessories in both men's homes...Islamic extremists are suspected...

"Islamic extremists my foot! I know who's doing this," Yolo grumbled as she watched the news. An odd mix of both pride and jealousy swept over her. "He's out having all the fun, while I'm stuck in the nest sitting on our egg."

"You are such an odd girl," Marquita laughed. She had replaced Mr. Grimsly as the voice of reason in her life.

"So!" Yolo poked out her lip and pouted. She hoisted herself off the sofa and waddled to her room. "Can't wait to have this baby so I can kill somebody."

****

"Islamic extremists my foot! I know who's doing this!" Doc spat angrily as he watched the same news report. It infuriated him that his old client got all the high profile cases.

He had just arrived in New York and as soon as he turned on the hotel TV there was Killa, again. Jealous rage and mental illness are not a good combination. Stir in a little good old fashion hating and you have a time bomb. That was Doc and he was about to implode.

"I got something that will get your attention. They won't be able to blame this on Islamic extremists!" he told his souvenir picture of Killa.

****

"Islamic extremists my foot! Last week a cat got stuck up a tree and they blamed Islamic extremists," Sincerity griped about the same report.

"I'll straighten it out," Killa said picking up his phone.

"Who you calling?" she frowned curiously.

"The police. Gonna let them know..."

"Just childish," Sincerity said taking the phone from him. "Speaking of snitches!" she growled when she saw the commotion in the courtyard.

Sincerity and half the project dwellers went to their windows to investigate. Killa too with his nosey ass.

"Shane home y'all!" Tito announced and picked him up by his waist as if he just scored a touchdown. In fact, he had just touched down from a bid upstate. He was being treated more like a celebrity than the snitch that he really was. Most people didn't know the whole story, but Sincerity did.

"Let me tell you 'bout this nigga," she hissed and began to lay it all out for him.

Shane was the project pretty boy, the resident Casanova. All the girls wanted to fuck him and all the dudes fucked with him because he got all the girls. He wasn't built for street life so the hood protected him. Especially Big BG and little BX. When Shane got robbed on 170th Street, they came to his rescue.

Technically, it wasn't even a robbery. Rocco slapped a spark out of the pretty boy for fucking his pretty sister. He slapped a lot of niggas over her because a lot of niggas had fucked her. He needed to grow two more hands to keep up with the demand. That's the law of supply and demand. If you met her demand to smoke a blunt, she would supply some pussy.

Shane was a pussy himself so when Rocco slapped him he emptied his pockets, and took off his jewelry and sneakers. Rocco shrugged and gladly accepted the spoils. He sent the sneakers upstairs, put the cash in his pocket, and the chain on his neck.

Had the courtyard been empty the coward would have snuck home and accepted his loss. But it wasn't, and he had to explain the handprint on his face along with his bare feet and neck.

"A-yo! I got robbed yo!" he lied as he rushed into the courtyard. "Them niggas pulled hammers on me and stole my shit!"

"Who? Ain't nobody takin' nothin' from nobody from University!" BG proclaimed proudly.

Somewhere in life, black people got life fucked up. Got tricked into claiming shit that wasn't theirs to claim. Blocks, corners, and sections of town they didn't own. Living, dying, and killing for what they could never possess. Streets that had been in existence a hundred years before them and would be there a hundred years after them. Yeah, somewhere in life some people got life fucked up.

"It was Rocco and dem. They took all my shit!" Shane retorted.

"Come on yo!" BG ordered. He passed gats to BX and Shane and led the charge over to 170th Street.

Of course, Rocco was out on the corner he claimed as his own. A couple of his workers served customers as they worked his package. None of them saw the approaching danger.

"There they go!" BX said pointing with his pistol.

BG raised his and they opened fire on the men. Shane didn't bust, he ran. Dropped his pistol and ran back to the projects. Rocco looked like he was pop locking when the bullets hit him. Once he finished his dance routine, he dropped dead. There would be no encore.

Police and paramedics came an hour later to claim the corpse. They scooped the dead man from his corner and put him in a bag. The next man had claimed that corner before they body bag was even zipped all the way closed.

Homicide detectives asked a few questions and got exactly what they expected, nothing. It was the Bronx and nobody was saying shit. Well, almost nobody.

Shane was so shook up he called the cops on himself the next morning. The desk sergeant actually hung up the call when he heard his claim. Around there, no one told on anyone, especially themselves. It had to be a prank caller.

Not to be denied, he marched down to the precinct and told them everything. He ended up with a gun charge while Big BG and little BX got murder charges. They even caught a pair of attempted murder for shooting a couple of bystanders who picked the wrong place to stand by.

Shane's statement helped convict his friends who tried to help him. They both got 25 to life while he got a skid bid of two years. Two years later, he returned to a hero's welcome because he went to prison. Ironically, Joey just got home from graduating college and didn't get shit.

"Sho nuff?" Killa giggled at the end of the story. What he found most amusing was the tone of her voice. It was murder. "Well if he's from here he knows the rules. Snitches get stiches and dumped in ditches," he recited the Bronx mantra as he stood. He didn't move yet because he knew what was coming. When it did come, he mouthed the words along with her.

"Let me do it," Sincerity insisted.

"Figured you'd say that. Grab my gun and come on. We'll drop the boys at Grandma's," he agreed.

"Nah, that's too quick. Too easy. That nigga needs to feel it. Just like my little cousin BX is feeling it," she growled.

"What you got in mind then?" he wondered.

"These," she replied slipping one of his brass knuckles over her dainty hand.

Dainty or not, she was Karate Joe's only daughter. He had taught her stuff he hadn't even taught the Dope Girl. Yeah, Sincerity was pretty, but she was pretty fucking dangerous as well. Shane's little ass was in trouble.

"How you gon' get him?" Killa inquired in amusement.

"That nigga been tryna fuck me for years. Today, I'ma say yes," she explained.

"Why you ain't tell me he tried to holla?" he retorted with a tinge of jealousy.

"For what? So you could kill him? Nigga you gonna need a nuke to kill errbody who tried to get at this," she teased giving her firm ass a slap.

"Have fun," he said plopping down and grabbing the remote. The world needs less snitches, he would gladly watch the kids while she purged.

****

"Bout time! I knew you was feeling a nigga! I knew it. The whole time I did that bid I was hoping you would be the first bitch I fucked when I got home. That's like that song by Verb. 'The First Bitch I Fucked.' Whatever happened to that nigga anyway?" Shane rambled excitedly.

He had every right to be excited when the project diva showed up at his door. Shane had his pick of any of the chicks he dicked before, but kicked them to the curb for Sincerity. His grandmother went to bingo leaving him home alone. He always said he was born alone and would die alone. He was right.

"Let's see what you working with. I ain't got all night," Sincerity insisted. To prove her point, she peeled off her painted on jeans. She had a head start but he still won the race to get naked.

"Dayum!" Shane shouted when he saw Sincerity completely naked. The two kids she bore spread her hips like strawberry jam. Her breasts were heavy with large brown nipples topping them off. He marveled at her round ass as she bent over to place her clothes in the hallway.

"So they won't get any blood on them," she explained.

"Blood?" Shane asked but didn't like the answer.

For a reply, she popped him right in his mouth. He opened his mouth to ask another question and got hit again. Sincerity wore brass knuckles on each hand and threw combinations that would make her eccentric father proud. She added knees and elbows as well adding insult to injury.

"Fucking snitch! Lil' BX doing time for your ass!" she asserted as she assaulted him.

He collapsed under the beating and she went with him. She beat him a full minute after he stopped breathing. Once the deed was done, she used his shower to clean his blood off and rushed home.

"Have fun?" Killa asked knowingly. He knew she would and knew what that meant. That's why he was butt naked on the sofa.

"That shit got me so hot!" Sincerity screamed as she shed her clothing. "Am I supposed to be this turned on?"

"It happens," he shrugged stroking himself erect as she stripped.

Sincerity rushed over to him and mounted him like a horse. As soon as he wiggled inside her, she rode off in search of a nut. She grudge fucked Killa until she found what she was looking for.

"Mutha...fucka!" she shouted when she came harder than any other time in her life. She fell off to the side panting to catch her breath.

"Oh no you don't," Killa laughed. She had gotten a nut and was ready to go to sleep. He acted as if he'd never done it to her.

Killa flipped the spent woman face down, ass up, and slid back inside her. She was too exhausted to throw it back, but didn't need to. A few chops later Killa was done himself.

"Muthafucka!" he agreed as he bust a nut of his own.

Once again, the couple fell asleep right there on the spot. Once again, Xavier was watching cartoons when they awoke.

Chapter 19

"Ok, ok, ok just be calm," Yolo instructed herself as she got up the nerve to make the call. She went through this every day and every day she chickened out. Not today, today was the day. She took a deep breath, held her chin high, and picked up the phone.

Yolo turned on the black mob phone and entered the security codes. With the security activated, the signal was untraceable. It would be routed all over the globe, switching networks every few seconds. Without the code, it was just a regular cell phone.

She checked herself in the mirror once more before dialing. Her hair was cute and her lips were glossed to a shine. Killa couldn't see her, but she still wanted to be cute for him. She was cute too with that healthy pregnant glow women get.

****

Killa stared at the ringing phone for a full minute just to make sure it was real. He had been hoping to get a call that could be traced so he could find the lunatic who murdered his son. He quickly activated the trace app and took the call. "Yes?"

"Hey bae! It's me...Yolo," she sang happily when the rather calm voice took the call. "Still mad at me?"

"Mad? Nah, why would I be?" he asked as he watched the signal jump from continent to continent. Have it tell it she was calling from Iraq.

"Miss me?" she asked hopefully. So hopefully that she crossed her fingers and held her breath as she waited for an answer.

"Of course I miss you. I want to see you," he lied causing Sincerity to pop straight up in bed.

"Miss who? Who you wanna see?" Sincerity barked as he scrambled to cover the receiver with his hand.

"Chill ma! It's Jake from State Farm," Killa quipped. It was too late though because the crazy chick had heard her.

"Ugh! I see that bitch is with you. Dang, I should have killed her when I had the chance. I have to kill her and the kids so we can be together...I love you, bye-bye," Yolo pouted and hung up.

****

"Mm hmm...that must be the baby daddy got you all in your feelings," Nurse Marquita observed catching the tail end of the conversation.

The observant lady knew something was special about that phone. Yolo kept it charged but never used it. No calls, no text, no games, likes, or pokes. Just fully charged and always off.

"His ass sitting up with some chick. Once I have his baby I'll have him all to myself," she said foolishly.

It was the baby mama mantra recited by a million baby mamas before her. It proved true for about twelve of them. Killa was catching some flack at the same time from his woman.

****

"Yolo huh? Yo' ass!" she huffed in frustration. It was bad enough he fucked the lunatic but did he have to knock her up?

"Yeah and I could have gotten her to meet me somewhere until you fucked it up," he shot back with his own frustration. "Damn jealous girlfriend shit!"

"What shit? Nigga I am a jealous girlfriend and when *we* catch up to that bitch *I'm* going to be the one to twist her shit!"

"She's a little tougher than Shane," he laughed. "Trust me, you ain't ready for Yolo!"

****

"You sure you don't want me to come? I don't mind you know. Don't be shy with me, I brought you into the world," Marquita fussed as Yolo prepared for her prenatal visit.

"I'm a big girl," she sulked. Yolo did not like being poked and prodded by doctors. She wanted a healthy child though so she manned up.

"Well, ok. I'm going to the market, you need anything?" the sweet lady offered.

Yolo smiled warmly at the only mother she'd ever known and declined. She knew the woman would buy her favorites anyway.

"See you later," she said kissing the woman's cheek. The two left in separate cars, heading in separate directions.

"Yolo Jackson," Yolo announced at the women's clinic reception desk.

"What a pretty name," the pretty receptionist complimented as she searched for her appointment. "You're a little early, but we had a cancellation so you can be seen now if you'd like.

"I like," she said slightly sarcastically.

The woman ignored it and directed her to an examination room. Yolo followed the directions and entered the crisp room. She saw the fresh gown on the exam table and changed into it but left her panties on. Those could wait for the doctor. As soon as she got on the table, the door opened and in walked a rather young black man.

"I'm supposed to have a woman doctor," she protested.

"She is. I'm the nurse. Just gotta check you out before she comes. Feet up please," he replied.

"Man," Yolo whined as she complied and put her feet in the stirrups. The gown on her knees prevented her from seeing exactly what he was doing down there. Good thing too.

"Oh you left your panties on," he said and pulled them aside. He snapped a few pictures with his phone. He then used two fingers to part her labia to get a little pink in his pictures. Then pushed his luck by pushing a finger inside. "Damn you tight!"

"Excuse me?" Yolo shot back indignantly. She had never heard a doctor or nurse say anything like that before.

"Um...I mean everything looks um... yeah the doctor will be in shortly," he stammered and rushed from the room.

A few minutes later the lady doctor waltzed in. "Oh?" she said surprised to see the patient in the stirrups. "We're just doing an ultrasound today so no need for that. You actually could have kept your clothes on."

"But the nurse..."

"Nurse! I wish I could afford a nurse. It's just Jen the receptionist, Jason the janitor, and me," she explained.

"Sho nuff?" Yolo said realizing she had been duped and molested. She wasn't even mad. If fact, she was quite pleased. Murder always made her giddy. It was just what the fake doctor ordered. Well, nurse and that's exactly what he was about to get. Murdered.

"Would you like to know the sex of your baby?" the doctor asked once she determined it on the screen.

"Um...no," she decided. She wanted to be surprised so she could call Killa and announce 'It's a boy' or 'It's a girl.'

"Everything looks great. Mom and baby are both healthy. Make sure you take your vitamins and..." the doctor rambled as Yolo got dressed.

"Thanks doc," she said appreciatively as she dressed. She missed most of the instructions thinking about her date for the evening.

"Do you have any hobbies? Something you like to do for fun?" the doctor asked.

"I do!" Yolo beamed happily. She knew better than to say what.

"Well make sure to do it. As much as possible. Happy moms make happy babies."

Yolo stepped out of the exam room and looked left, right, and left again like she was trying to cross the street. Except she wasn't looking for cars, she wanted to find that janitor.

Jason came out of the janitor's closet winded from busting a nut. They didn't get too many young black women in the clinic so he couldn't wait to get off until he got off. He went into his supply room and used the medical lubricant to masturbate. He flinched when he saw Yolo like he was about to run. He was until she flashed her pretty smile at him. He took the bait, smiled back, and approached.

"I think you tricked me," Yolo giggled like it was no big deal. Like she wasn't going to brutally murder the man for violating her.

"I um, I'm going to school to be a doctor too. I just be tryna get some practice," he lied. Jason was going to upload those pictures to a pervert site dedicated to stolen crotch shots. A community of freaks took up skirt and under table pictures of women and shared them online.

"Oh! Ok, that makes sense. Why don't I come to your house so you can take your time and get some practice?" she offered sweetly. Yolo was helpful like that.

"Really? Yes, hell yes!" Jason cheered. He quickly scribbled his address and skipped happily down the hall. The rest of the day dragged by slowly. Luckily, it was his last day on the job. Last day on the planet.

****

Jason spent the last few hours of his life getting his little apartment tidy for his murderer. He vacuumed, dusted, and jacked off once more. Just to take the edge off if he got lucky. He didn't get lucky too often and wanted it to last. His luck with real women was pretty bad but he was quite the stud.

He wasn't the only one masturbating. Yolo had been tortured by her two fetishes lately. For one, she hadn't bust a nut in months and was overdue. She played with her love button until the dam broke.

"Damn!" she exclaimed at the strong orgasm that made her legs quiver. That was one thirst quenched. Now she needed to murder something. Good thing for her some pervert popped into her life and offered his for sacrifice.

"Eenie, meenie, minee...moe," the childish murderer sang as she selected a murder weapon. A cute .22 revolver got the call and was placed in her purse.

"And just where are you going young lady?" Marquita wanted to know. "All gussied up."

"I'm not," Yolo giggled. The cute, knee length skirt and sandals were far from gussied up. Especially with the baby bump sticking out in the middle.

"Well at least I don't have to worry about you getting pregnant," she huffed. Marquita lifted her face to accept the kiss on her cheek. A smile spread on her face as she watched the girl depart.

Jason paced like a caged lion as he waited for his date. He planned to brag far and wide if he got some ass. Of course, he would leave out the pregnant part. The pictures he'd uploaded already were a big hit with his fellow perverts. He hoped to have a few more to share later.

"Yes!" he cheered pumping his fist at the sound of his doorbell. He got a little lightheaded from the excitement and sudden erection. When he pulled it open, there stood Yolo.

"I hope you know how to eat pussy," she announced as she rushed past him. She marched straight over to the sofa and sat back.

"I, I, I," he stuttered when she pulled her skirt up and cocked her legs on the coffee table.

"I, I, I hope that's a y, y, yes," she snapped as she pulled off her moist panties.

He was no pro, but eating pussy is pretty much self-explanatory. Her hisses and moans guided him along. Soon, he was twirling his tongue like a champ. Yolo tried her best to fight off an orgasm, which only made it worse.

"Fuck!" she screamed as the ecstasy wracked her body. Jason clamped down on that clam and sucked out the gravy.

"So, how'd I do?" he asked confidently as she still shook.

"Great! So good that I almost hate to do this," she replied as she dug in her purse.

"Do what?" Jason asked and got shot in his face for a reply.

The impact of the bullet knocked Jason onto the table. He rolled off and tried to make a run for it but a calf shot dropped him. When he stuck his hand up to block, he got shoot through it.

"I haven't...killed anyone...in months," Yolo said between shots to his face and neck. By the time the gun was empty, so was his body. His soul seeped out one of the many bullet holes leaving the empty shell behind.

"That was fun, but I need to see my baby," Yolo pouted. She decided to take a trip into the city to see if she could at least see him. Decided to bring a rifle too just in case she saw his baby mama or kids.

Yolo cleaned up traces of her being in Jason's apartment as best she could. She did bust a nut in his mouth, but he could keep that. Before she left, she took a few picture of him and uploaded them to the site. The caption read, 'Hot Date.'

Chapter 20

Killa and Sincerity had just completed one of their sexual triathlons. It consisted of a mutually beneficial 69, followed by a pony ride, and wrapped up face to face with her ankles on his shoulders. They crossed the finish line within seconds of each other.

It was time to bask in the after sex glow. For Sincerity, it meant caressing her man while humming Mary J. Blige tunes. Meanwhile, Killa hit a blunt from the ashtray. He took a deep pull and held the smoke so the THC could seep into his blood stream. When he exhaled, he blew thick smoke rings and watched them waft towards the ceiling. It was all good until a commotion outside in the courtyard interrupted the night.

"A-yo!" Y'all muthafuckas get up and hear what we got to say!" a young teen demanded from atop the playground monkey bars.

Killa rolled out of bed and went to the window to investigate with his nosey ass. He wasn't the only one though. Half of the residents had filled their windows to hear the proclamation.

Ju-Ju waited on his audience before he continued. A group of ten more boys, barely in their teens milled around ready to co-sign his every word. Killa laughed at the mean mugs on their hairless boyish faces.

"Yo we the N.G.G. and this is our world! If you wanna live in it, you gotta pay. Sell weed, coke, pussy, you gotta pay. Use the elevators you gotta pay. You live in these projects you gotta pay."

"Is he high?" Killa asked with a frown. "The fuck is an N.G.G.?"

"Yes he is high but he's serious!" Sincerity lamented. "They call themselves the New Generation Goons."

"Goons? My old gang? Fuck they talking about, we were good kids, fucking boy scouts," he recalled fondly.

"Boy stop," Sincerity laughed. Cracked up actually at the outlandish and inaccurate recollection. "I was here, remember?"

"Ok yeah we sold a little drugs, killed a few people, but we didn't fuck with civilians," he replied.

That statement was almost true except they sold a lot of drugs and killed a lot of people. Only they did not fuck civilians. Getting robbed is a hazard of the drug trade. It's expected and accepted but regular people were off limits. That was written in stone and respected.

"Well these little fucks don't respect nothing or no one. They getting worse and worse since little Self left," she explained.

Explained correctly too. Ever since Self went to Atlanta with Cameisha, the gang he once led lost direction. They lost their hustle and got lazy. They were definitely new generation goons. Too lazy to sell drugs so they robbed the addicts before they could spend with the dealers. That meant the dealers had to pay sales tax to allow the sales to come through.

The weed man had to donate free weed and the crack whores chipped in free blowjobs. Papi at the bodega had to turn a blind eye to the little bastards when they pillaged his aisles. If not, out came the guns and gone went the day's receipts. Better to let the fuckers steal beer and food. They had real fun looting and terrorizing the projects. Real fun indeed until along came a Killa.

"I guess I better go talk to him huh?" Killa sighed billowing weed smoke.

"Not him, them," Sincerity hissed. She was sick of the feral boys and wanted them gone. All of them.

"Nah, them dudes is followers. Trust me, they ain't tryna follow their leader where he's going," he surmised. Sincerity gave him a hug that led to a kiss that led to round two.

****

"So I hear you got rats," Killa said as he took a seat next to Nitty on the park bench. He turned his nose up at the extended blunt and waved it off. Nitty shrugged like 'more for me.'

"Little rat bastards you mean," he griped and hit the blunt again. "These little fuckas getting outta hand."

On cue, several of the youngsters chased a man into the courtyard and beat him. Luckily, the kids were too light in the ass to do any damage. It was just too many to fight off, so he covered up and took their punches and kicks.

"Let me catch you on the elevator again without paying tax," Ju-Ju warned explaining the infraction he was getting beat for. Once they finished, he turned and locked eyes with Killa. The boy cocked his head arrogantly.

"Is this dude serious?" Killa laughed and let him win the staring contest.

Ju-Ju nodded as if he had done something. He wasn't old enough to fully understand why no one fucked with him or his family. The older people spoke of Killa in hushed tones when they did speak of him. Ju-Ju pointed at them and two young goons marched over.

"I was gonna let them enjoy their weekend," Killa said as he scanned the courtyard to see who was about to witness a murder.

"A-yo, Nitty, we need that bench tax homie," Raheem announced careful not to make eye contact with the legend.

"Here!" Nitty grumbled and broke the kid off a wad of cash from one of the wads of cash in his pockets. The other kid snatched it and scurried off as Killa stared in shock.

"You too?" he exclaimed.

"Son, it's either pay the tax or they fuck with the customers. They make it so hot no one wants to come shop. They used to work for me until that fuck Ju-Ju turned up!"

"Well Ju-Ju is about to turn up dead. Get ready to get your employees back," Killa said as he stood to leave.

"They getting a pay cut!" Nitty yelled after him.

****

"Fuck you doing in here!" a young goon barked when Killa barged into the rec center they used as headquarters. The same one the original goons commandeered many years earlier.

"Whoa! Easy, easy," Killa advised. He raised his hands and did a little twirl to show he was unarmed.

"What's in the bag? Better be for me!" Ju-Ju said with a snarl he couldn't back up. Since all his goons had guns, he didn't need to carry one.

"As a matter of fact, it is for you," he said as it was snatched from his hand. The doorman rushed it over to his boss.

Ju-Ju turned the bag over and frowned at the contents that dropped in front of him. A thick leather belt caught everyone's attention since everyone had gotten their ass whipped by one similar. A shiny metal ring rolled out last.

"Fuck is this yo?" Ju-Ju demanded.

"Put it over your head...Ok now hit the switch," Killa directed and the curious kid complied.

"This switch?" Ju-Ju asked as he hit it. He didn't get to hear the answer because his head separated from the rest of his body. The body sat back down on the chair and the head rolled away.

"That's the one," Killa chuckled and picked up the belt. "Ok the rest of y'all put your guns down and line up."

Seeing Ju-Ju get his head cut off was all they needed to see. They sat their guns down and got in a single file line. One by one, Killa whooped each of their asses. After spanking the kids, he sent them to Nitty to work off what they'd extorted.

Chapter 21

The University Projects in the Bronx, New York was zero percent white. There were plenty of blacks, Latinos, Haitians, and Jamaicans but not a single solitary white person. It was even too far from any suburbs for white customers to come cop. That meant that any white person who came through was on some sort of official business. That meant they were not to be fucked with, period.

Don't rob them; don't try to sell them drugs, pussy, nothing. Leave them the fuck alone. That's why no one gave the little white man a second glance as he ambled through the courtyard. They saw him then turned away as if they hadn't seen him. Only one set of eyes followed him but that was through the scope of a high-powered rifle from a near-by rooftop.

"Is that the fuckin' guy?" Yolo wondered aloud as it hit her where she knew him from. That was the same guy Killa got in trouble for not killing. She tightened her finger around the trigger to shoot, but curiosity got the best of her.

"Just what are you up to?" she mused when she saw what building he went into.

"How can I help you?" Nitty asked when Doc got out of the elevator.

"Yes, I'm here to call upon a Mrs....Forrest?" he replied sounding professional. Even reading the name from a file as if it were a formal business visit.

"Follow me," he advised and turned to lead the way down the hall. As soon as his back was turned, Doc slipped the DC 2000 over his head and hit the switch. The head did a back flip and landed right in Doc's hand. The body kept on marching down the hall without it.

"Who is it?" Diedra called through her door. When no reply came, she looked through the peephole and saw Nitty's face. That disarmed her enough to open the door. You should have seen her face when she saw Doc holding the head up to the peephole.

"Shit!" he muttered when the hard to shock woman passed out cold. He had hoped to snatch the lady and leave. That way he could make Killa come to him.

"Argh! What the..." Diedra gagged and coughed when Doc doused her with cold water.

"You're coming with me. Scream and I hit the switch," he warned as he helped her to her feet.

"Ok, I won't scream. Can I get my purse?" she pleaded.

"Why not? Especially since I got this out of it," Doc said holding up the tiny two shot pistol she carried. "Now come on!"

"Poor baby," Grandma moaned seeing Nitty at the end of the hall. Doc had sat him up in the corner and put his head on crooked. He walked the woman out holding the DC 2000 around her neck like a leash.

"Where the hell did you get that from," Yolo moaned when she saw the deadly device. Typical girl shit, wants to be the only one with the latest fashion. She quickly packed up her gun and made it downstairs. Doc had a head start on her, but she quickly caught up with him on the bridge going back over to Manhattan, and then followed them out to Queens.

****

"Oh what now? The little old lady who cried wolf," Killa complained when the satellite phone began to ring. The vintage Biggie Smalls ringtone told him who it was before looking at the screen. "What happened now Grandma? A bird messed on your window? Want me to kill all the pigeons until we find out which one? Or the newsboy was late again? Guess I should shoot him too."

"Actually I've been kidnapped Mr. Smarty Pants," Diedra huffed indignantly. As if, she hadn't asked her grandson to shoot the tardy newspaper boy in his ass. On more than one occasion.

"Say wha..." Killa tried to ask but the line went dead. He called right back and got nothing. The same results came from calling her house and cell phone.

"What's wrong?" Sincerity asked reading the distress in his brows.

"Not sure," he replied snatching his boots on and rushing towards the door.

"Sup Unc?" Raheem asked as Killa marched towards his grandmother's building.

"A- yo, you see a pregnant chick around here?" he asked.

"Unc it's mad pregnant chicks out here," the kid laughed. It was the end of cuffing season, which always results in a bunch of pregnant chicks and dudes in denial.

"Nah, one that ain't from here," Killa specified.

"I ain't seen no one that ain't from here around here," Raheem replied to his departing back. He had seen Doc when he came but it just didn't register.

"This nigga," Killa fumed seeing Nitty sitting in the corner. He initially thought he was laying down on the job until he noticed that it wasn't the man's fitted cap that was crooked. It was his head.

Killa whipped out his pistol and keys. He entered the apartment gun first like the police.

"Grandma! Grandma?" he called from empty room to empty room until his search came up empty. There was no sign of a struggle and her purse lay open minus the gun she kept. He hung his head in defeat as he crossed back through the courtyard.

"What babe?" Sincerity asked on the verge of tears. She had never seen her man that worried and it worried her.

"Yolo took my grandmother. That crazy bitch is going to kill her," he said coming to grips with his failure.

"That's it! I'm going to kill that bitch myself! Oh I ain't gon' fuck her first though! I'ma make sure she's dead!" she spat.

Killa listened to her rant and rave without reply. Instead, he pulled a suitcase and began to put her clothes in it. Sincerity frowned curiously and finally asked, "What are you doing?"

"Packing. You and the kids are going to South America. I'm going to find that girl and kill her. I can't be worried about you guys.

Sincerity started to protest but recognized the no protest look on his face. She sucked her teeth in defiance and started packing clothes for the boys. Time paused when the Black Mob phone began to ring. The sound seemed to freeze Killa in place.

"Answer it!" she shouted unfreezing him

"Where...is...she?" Killa growled so deeply the room vibrated.

"Damn you got a sexy voice," Yolo gushed as the fumble from his voice sent shock waves through her body. She felt a shiver that soaked her big maternity panties. "I didn't take her but I know where she is."

"Where?" he screamed then frowned dubiously at the answer. It made absolutely no sense. Add the fact that he was dealing with a lunatic and he really didn't know what to think.

"You believe her?" Sincerity questioned when he relayed the information. Before he could reply, Biggie started rapping again.

"Hello, Grandma?" he asked hopefully.

"J.F.K. Gate 10," Diedra said stoically as if reading from a script. The line went dead instantly.

"Why the airport?" Sincerity frowned.

"The bitch knows I can't bring a gun, a knife...shit, I can't even bring a pair of fingernail clippers!" he snapped.

Yolo realized the same thing when she trailed Doc to the airport. He walked Diedra in with a scarf around the device on her neck. The TSA agents were too busy looking for Islamic extremists to even notice. Instead, they searched a Muslim couple's belongings. Even went through their baby's diaper and came up with shit.

Not wanting to be unarmed herself, Yolo had to think quickly. She did just that when she saw an old woman in a wheelchair complete with oxygen tank.

"Excuse me ma'am," Yolo sang sweetly as the woman pulled a tote bag from her car trunk.

"Yes dear?" the woman asked displaying her dentures.

"I need your wig, chair, and oxygen tank. Please," she replied.

The old lady chuckled at what she thought was a joke until Yolo strangled her with the oxygen tubing. She quickly removed her wig and dress before rolling the woman under her own car. She put on the woman's dress and wig before climbing into her chair. The woman's knitting needles gave her a bright idea. She turned the pressure all the way down in the oxygen tank and jammed the needle inside of the tubing. All she had to do now was turn the valve and she had a spear gun.

"Think, think, think," Killa repeated as he made his way through the terminal. By the eighth gate, he still hadn't come up with a plan.

He still couldn't figure out why Yolo would bring her here. They couldn't do anything and get away with it in the busy airport full of security. It wasn't just crazy; it was stupid and didn't fit. As soon as he reached gate 10, he got his answer.

"Xavier," Grandma Diedra called out and waved until Doc snatched her hand down.

"You? Why won't anyone stay dead?" Killa asked as he sat across from Doc and his grandmother. The madman had his fingers on the switch that would decapitate the woman.

"Chief Flores stayed dead," Doc shot back proudly. "I'm pretty sure she will too once her head comes off!"

"Then what? Just walk away?" Killa asked trying to make sense of why they were there.

"Then we fight to the death!" Mano a mano. No guns or bombs. The winner will be famous!" Doc said with the far away gaze of a madman.

"We..." Killa began then paused when his attention was stolen. Even in disguise, he recognized the lunatic rolling up behind Doc. He got even more confused as to why she was there. He got his answer a second later.

Yolo looked straight ahead, as she rolled behind the rambling Doc. Once she was close enough, she lifted her makeshift gun and turned the valve. The knitting needle entered the base of Doc's brain and killed him instantly. Right in the middle of another dumb statement.

"Bastard!" Diedra grumbled as she removed the bootleg DC 2000 from her neck. She rushed to her grandson and into his arms.

"Even Steven?" Yolo asked hopefully with her crazy ass.

"Not even close. You killed my son," he replied through clenched teeth. "First chance I get, I'm going to kill you."

"Or me, you," she giggled. "Either way, it'll be a beautiful death."

Epilogue

Yolo stole a long, loving glance as she rolled away. Killa stuck his middle finger up in reply. As much as he wanted to murder her, there was nothing he could do. Imagine choking a pregnant chick in the middle of J.F.K. airport.

"Let's bounce yo," Diedra said snatching his attention away from the lunatic.

"Yeah before someone notices he's not sleeping," he replied looking down at the dead doctor. The DC 2000 suddenly snapped shut on its own, causing Diedra to rub her neck where it had been for hours.

"Please tell me that's not your baby," she said as they rushed from the terminal.

"Huh?" he shot back as he'd done his whole life causing the woman who knew him his whole life to shake her head. Once outside, he hailed a taxi. "LaGuardia!"

"Where are we going?" Diedra demanded when she heard the name of the next airport.

"We, nowhere. You, South America. Sincerity and the boys are on the way already. You guys are staying there until this is over. Until she's dead."

Diedra blew her breath in protest but kept quiet. She knew him well enough to know she couldn't talk him out of it anyway. She pouted and poked her lip out all the way through the next airport. Her lip was still poked out as her plane climbed into the sky.

****

"Team one in place," a gunman announced into his walkie-talkie.

"Team two ready," the next gunman gave his reply. The man running the teams took a second to bask in victory before giving the command.

"See what happens when you fuck with the Black Mob?" Big Rock gloated.

Once Baron and Casper's deaths were discovered, a power struggle ensued for control of the powerful crime family. Big Rock had the best killers and came out on top. It was no secret that Killa had killed them, but no dead Yolo meant she was involved. It took a while to track them but since neither activated their security on the last call, both phones were tracked to the last location. At the same time that Killa and Yolo were face to face in the airport, gunmen arrived at their homes. I guess you can't really call them gunmen with what they were packing.

"Fire!" Big Rock commanded dramatically.

Marquita had just walked to the large plate glass window to investigate the car that was parked in front of the house. Just as she opened the curtains, the masked man pulled the trigger. The grenade launcher made a poof sound as it lobbed the high explosive device. The nurse was blown into hundreds of pieces along with her home.

Simultaneously in the Bronx Team One fired from the courtyard into Sincerity and Grandma's apartments. Luckily, they were both over the Atlantic Ocean when their apartments were destroyed. Team One pulled pistols and murdered Raheem and three other kids who were outside.

Both Yolo and Killa arrived at their respective residences and found the carnage. Diedra and Sincerity may have been the targets, but ten others died in the Bronx attack. Neighbors on each side of their apartments died in the blast along with the four kids shot in the courtyard.

"This crazy bitch!" Killa growled and pulled out the Black Mob phone.

"Oh you went too far!" Yolo spat when she saw police putting pieces of the nurse in little yellow bags. She too pulled out her Black Mob phone.

"Hello?" both Killa and Yolo asked hearing a man's laughter on the line before they got a chance to dial.

"I thought it was good-bye," Big Rock chuckled. "Bet we don't miss you next time!"

"Who the fuck was that?" Killa asked once he clicked off.

"The same person who tracked these phones. Meet me where we met!" Yolo replied urgently.

They both tossed the now worthless phones and retraced their steps. An hour later, they were back at gate 10 at J.F.K. Doc was still there looking like he was sleeping.

"Just tell me who they are and where they're at," Killa stated.

"You can't take them on. They're too many and too powerful," Yolo explained. "Protect me until I have the baby and we'll kill them together."

Killa pondered her suggestion. As much as he hated to admit it, she was right. He would need her help. "I want to kill all of them. Every member, in every city!"

"Hells yeah! You and me! Killa and Yolo! Let's give them all a beautiful death!"

The End.

PAPERBACK TITLES

DOPE GIRL

DOPE GIRL 2

DOPE GIRL 3

THE PREACHERS WIFE

SHAWTS

YUNG PIMPIN

eBOOKS

LIL MISS MOLLY
JACK & ILL
YUNG PIMPIN
CRYSTAL METH
KILLA
KILLA SEASON
STUD
RA & DRE
THE SHAHADAH

Coming Soon

WITCHES OF THE WEST END
REVEREND CASH
BAD COP
THE SOCIAL NETWORK

JACK & ILL

"Mmmmm Janice, you like this dick? Tell me you like this th...hold up..." Mike paused to put himself back inside his newest conquest. It kept slipping out of her every time he tried to get a good stroke going.

"Ok there we go.....yeah! Tell me you like this dick!" he demanded.

"Yeah it's good, you're the best," Jackie said dryly. She was glad he chose to hit her from the back so he couldn't see the *'yeah right'* look on her face.

Jackie couldn't decide what was worse, the tiny dick or the motor mouth. Big Mike as he was called ran a booming drug crew out of the Polo Grounds in Harlem and was seeing major cake. His team moved weed, coke and X in large amounts. Yet for all his street savvy and business acumen there were two things big Mike could not do.

The first thing was fuck. Nature played a cruel joke on the handsome 6'4" man by giving him a four-inch dick. And he obviously didn't know or understand how small he was because he kept trying positions that were out of his dick range.

The second thing that Mike absolutely, positively could not do was shut the fuck up! Dude began talking as soon as his eyes opened in the morning and ran his mouth until he went to sleep and beyond. If he couldn't get it all out during the day, he would just talk in his sleep. Some chicks would just leave in the middle of the night to escape the onslaught.

He talked so much that he often told total strangers all his business. That's how he ended up in the position he was currently in. No, not hitting Jackie's perfect ass from behind, but what came along with it.

'Must be going for a new record' Jackie mused to herself as a glance at the clock indicated he was closing in on two minutes inside of her.

"Whose pussy is thi...thi....arg!" Big Mike grunted cumming up just short of his own three-minute record. "Whose pussy is this?" he gasped between gulps of air.

"Mine nigga!" Ill Will announced as he stepped fully into the room.

"Who the fuck is you?" Mike asked into the barrel of the huge desert eagle staring down at him.

"Oh Mike this is Will. Will, Mike," Jackie said as she climbed from under the big man and off the large poster bed.

"You know him?" Big Mike asked, ignoring the obvious.

"Yeah that's Ill Will, my boyfriend. He's a robber," she replied, pulling her panties back on as Mike, even in the predicament he was in, still watched lustfully.

"Damn babe, you said dude had a small dick but damn!" Will laughed holding his prey at cannon point.

"A-yo B, you ain't gotta dis me! If you gone rob me, then rob me. No sense putting a nigga down," Big Mike said wounded.

"Tie that cry baby up," Will demanded as Jackie finished dressing. She quickly complied and secured his hands behind him with plastic ties.

Jackie then went into his closet and retrieved a satchel full of money that he showed her earlier. Big Mike made that same mistake of showing off his money to every chic he brought home. He bragged about it to 'Janice' the first night he met her and she coyly set him up to see it. That is was she did. Jack and Ill were stick up kids.

DOPE GIRL 1, 2, & 3

Cameisha was all girl, but she definitely had balls. She boarded the plane with four ounces of cocaine tucked snuggly in her panties. Taking it on the plane made it a federal charge but that was even better. Any criminal would much rather do time in a comfy fed joint than in a fucked up state prison.

Tommy seemed to love the synthetic coke but now it was time for some human trials. High Bridge Projects had hundreds of test subjects who would pay to sample the product. When Cameisha deplaned in New York, Deidra was at the gate waiting. She braced herself for a grandma hug. Only a bear hug from an actual grizzly bear packed more power. Plenty of grand kids had been snapped in half by grandma hugs.

"Cameisha!" Deidra screamed like a groupie at the sight of her beloved granddaughter. She rushed over pretty quickly for a woman her age and scooped her into her arms.

"Hey Grandma," Cameisha blurted as all the air left her body.

Deidra released her death grip and inspected Cameisha. When she was satisfied that she was intact, she led the way out of the terminal. The only baggage she carried was the carry-on since she planned to shop while she was there. What's a trip to New York without a shopping spree?

The car service provided a large luxury sedan to ferry Mrs. Forrest to and from the airport. The polite driver stole Cameisha's heart instantly by being so sweet. The elderly man held the door open for the ladies just like a gentleman is supposed to. The girls sank back into the plush leather seats and made girl talk all the way uptown. Once the car crossed the bridge into the Bronx, Cameisha switched to high alert.

Again, she regretted not killing E-man instead of just beating him. He of course blamed the attack on some teens in the projects and had them murdered. Of course he wasn't going to admit he got his ass whooped by some girls. He now had to wear a fitted cap to hide all of the stitches he got from the beating that night.

Meisha stared at the corner of 164th street as the car glided up the hill on Ogden Avenue. She was hoping that he wouldn't be outside but no such luck. There was E-man and a couple of his cronies having a board meeting on the corner. She could have ducked her head and hid but grandpa never taught that lesson. No surrender, no retreat. Had she been armed, she would have gunned him down on the spot. Since she didn't have any bullets, she shot daggers instead.

"A'ight, y'all niggas spread out and cut off all traffic up the hill. If a nigga tryna get high, don't let him by!" E-man said directing his workers. He was looking in all directions pointing out spots for them to trap when he saw the luxury car. When he and Meisha made eye contact, it took a two count for him to place the face. By three, he pulled a gun from his waist and raised it.

"Drive!" Cameisha yelled as she pulled her grandmother to the floor and dove on top of her. The driver didn't need to be told twice and floored the car just as gunfire erupted. He let out a grunt when one of the nine-millimeter rounds went through the door and into his torso. E-man ran out into the street dumping at the car as it sped away. His crew was so stunned by the sudden violence they showed up late and got off a few harmless shots. Harmless or not, they were going to cost them their lives.

The driver slumped over the wheel once his clock stopped. The car slowed by sideswiping parked cars before coming to a complete stop against a street light.

"Are you hit?" Cameisha asked frantically searching her grandmother for gunshot wounds.

"I'm fine, let's get out of her!" Deidra shouted and got out of the crumpled car. " What the hell was that?"

"I don't know. You ain't beefing with nobody are you?" Cameisha lied as they rushed towards the projects.

"Some broad was talking mess cuz I 'liked' her man's picture but...I know one thing; your uncle will get to the bottom of it today!"

"Wait, Killa is here?" Meisha asked excited to finally meet the myth of a man.

"That's right, Killa's here!"

KILLA

Introduction

Xing Lee was talking cash shit as the good doctor stroked away at her hairless box. She was 'oohing' and 'aahing' and cursing in her native tongue as her current lover loved her. For all he knew she was talking bad about him but he didn't speak Vietnamese so it sounded as good as it felt.

"Me love you long time!" Doc grunted as he slammed into her. His love life had greatly improved since his miserable wife died at the hands of the country's most dangerous killer known as Killa.

The doctor was treated as a hero after surviving the home invasion that claimed his beloved wife. A minor celebrity to all except his wife's family. They blamed him for his former patient taking her life.

Doc now had quite a few girlfriends on payroll, but Xing was by far his favorite. He currently had her on her side in the scissor position and was giving her the business. He was four and a half inches deep pounding away. His prim and prissy wife would have never let him put her in a position like this. Whenever she did feel benevolent enough to part with a little vagina, it was one way. From the back while laying on her side so she wouldn't have to look at him. There was no kissing, no talking, and no tenderness. Just hurry up and get off and get off.

When the doctor's stroke grew choppy, Xing threw it into overdrive. She began moaning and thrashing around as if he was slaying it. He wasn't, she was just a good actor. Her performance helped doc reach an intense orgasm he no doubt would tip for.

Xing was bright enough to at least let her lover think he was knocking it out the park. The key to a man's heart is his ego, not stomach. Any stranger can fill your belly, but making a middle-aged man feel vibrant was more important. She may or may not have had an orgasm along with him. It's hard to tell with professionals, or wives.

"Ooh doctor you number one G.I! You love me long time!" Xing said quite believably as she got up from the bed. She rushed into the bathroom and under the shower. She was back minutes later and quickly dressed. A kiss on the forehead served as goodbye and she was gone.

"I'm an animal!" Doc cheered, beating on his chest like King Kong. It's one of the silly things people do when they think they're alone, only he wasn't.

"Lion or tiger?" a voice asked from the shadows.

Ordinarily the ordinary man would have been frightened at the presence of an uninvited stranger in his home but he wasn't. He actually smiled at the sound of the voice he knew well. Uninvited he may have been but he was no stranger.

"A lion, I'm king of the fucking jungle!" he laughed as his now welcome guest stepped from the shadows and into view. "How long have you been here?"

"Long enough to see you and your buddy bumping uglies. Oh, and I speak Korean. She was saying you have a little dick and your elbow was pulling her hair."

"Fuck you Killa, she's Vietnamese!" Doc laughed cracking them both up. "Let me put something on."

Killa turned away when the doctor bounded out of the bed in his pinkish birthday suit.

"You're looking trim, no homo," he complimented.

"None taken, thank you," doc said proudly as he headed into his bathroom to wash his and Xing's body fluids off him. When he returned he found the room empty. He almost called out in fear until he smelled his guest in the other room. Killer had found his way to the den and poured a shot of cognac to go along with his blunt. Doc found him laying back in a recliner blowing smoke rings from the pungent weed.

"So what brings you back to town? I assumed you would be in Brazil or Belize by now. It's been what, a year?" the doctor asked as he poured a shot of his own.

"Back? Shit I never left. I love Atlanta," Killa replied. He extended the blunt to his host out of courtesy and to his surprise; the doctor took it and took a healthy pull.

"A lot's changed," Killa said noting the new life in the older man.

"Well yeah! I've changed everything," the doctor replied between tokes. He assumed Killa meant the new decor of the house not his new demeanor. The weight loss, the tan, the, weed smoking it took his wife's death for him to live.

"I feel like a new man, I'm alive!" doc cheered.

"Yeah well murder will do that. Why you think I'm always so fucking happy," Killa chuckled.

"Been killing much?" doc asked enthusiastically.

"Have I!" he shot back animatedly at the gross understatement.

"Tell me about, please!" the doctor gushed eagerly and adjusted himself to get comfortable for the ride. He leaned back on his chaise to enjoy the story totally unaware he would be a part of it.

The Preacher's Wife

Prologue

How the hell did I get here? Teresa wondered inwardly as she glanced up at the giggling teenager standing over her.

If the act wasn't sad enough, she also had to contend with the young man's vulgar speech and sweaty balls slapping at her chin.

"Dat's right! Suck dat dick bitch! Eat it ho!" Lil Red demanded as he humped her face. Technically, it couldn't be called a blowjob because the vile little boy was literally fucking her face.

Teresa gagged loudly each time he slammed into her larynx. Her full mouth forced her to inhale the flavor of nuts that had missed at least two showers, and in the sweltering Atlanta heat, that was not a good idea.

Just hurry, Teresa sighed, *and do not...cu....Ewww! He's cumming in my mouth!*

"Mmm take it bitch! Eat! Eat!" Lil Red giggled as he skeeted on her tonsils. Teresa had no choice but to swallow the pulses of bitter semen since her head was held firmly in place.

"Dayum you got some fire ass head!" The man-child exclaimed, taking a few final humps before extracting himself from her mouth.

"Thank you, you're too kind," Teresa replied sarcastically but the quip was wasted on the ignorant young dealer.

"Here you go shawty," Lil Red said, extending his open palm filled with dime size pieces of crack. The young veteran had cut the drug at angles that made it appear more than it actually was. Still, five dimes was a lot for some head.

The local junkies will go as low as four dollars in a pinch. But this was no local junky. Her SUV, clothes, and even her smell spoke money, yet she had none. Lil Red didn't think she would accept his crass proposal to "suck a nigga dick" but she did.

Teresa looked at the drugs with dismay. She felt like slapping the poison across the room. However, a far more intense urge insisted she pluck them from his hand.

"Shit fall through tomorrow, I'll let you suck this dick again," Lil Red offered politely over his shoulder as he exited the hotel room.

As soon as he crossed the threshold of the door, Teresa ran to secure it. She loathed the ghetto of Atlanta, but crack cocaine was not sold in her upscale suburban neighborhood.

She quickly removed one of the rocks from its tiny plastic bag and spilt it in two. After loading one-half onto her straight shooter, she quickly followed it up with a flame.

"*Ahhh!*" Teresa exclaimed when she finally exhaled that overdue hit. She deserved it too for all she does. Daughter Hazel was at ballet class and son Calvin was at soccer, this was "me time."

Her free hours were spent devouring the drugs she purchased with her dignity. Then it was time to return to her life, "Life as the Preachers Wife."

LIL MISS MOLLY

Hazel didn't fare much better on her first day at Washington High school. It was named after Denzel, not George. Since there were more kids out of school then in, several schools were closed and combined. They closed schools and built prisons.

The violent, drug infested school was too far to walk to so she walked to the bus stop. Students were given free passes to ride the city buses. Like her brother, she was in some shit before she even reached school.

"Who dis bitch?" a girl frowned as Hazel approached.

"Oh she think she cute!" another observed. And she was cute even in the school uniform.

The city of Atlanta wisely opted to force kids to wear uniforms so students would be dressed uniformly. You know the cool ghetto kids had to pimp their clothes. The boys wore the pants a couple of sizes up and hanging off their asses. The girls hemmed skirts to mid-thigh or low crotch and half button shirts to show cleavage.

Hazel's uniform was worn properly at the knee and buttoned to her neck. It was the matching Coach bag and shoes that got her hated on. Then the ratchet girls couldn't see any weave hump and really got mad. This chick had the nerve to have real hair! How dare her! Bitch!

Hazel tried to ignore the girls and cracked a half smile at a pretty brown girl covered except for her cute face. The girl cracked a duplicate half smile and turned back to the remembrance of her lord. She used the finger of her right hand and moved her lips.

The girls loudly ridiculed her the entire ride to school. Having English first period brought a smile to Hazels face. This was her favorite subject, until now that is.

"Hey y'all, it's mi mall and I's yo' teacher fo' first period English," said a young woman who looked like something out of a low budget rap video. She had red weave piled high on her head and dressed like a hoochie mama.

"You cannot be serious!" Hazel said hotly. "You aren't even speaking English!"

"Yes I'm is!" the teacher shot back while moving her neck back and forth like only a ghetto girl can.

"Dat bitch dink she betta dan us!" a student demanded from the back.

Hazel may have fared better had she not opened her mouth. Now she had everyone's full attention. All eyes were now upon the pretty, brown girl, with thick brown hair. The boys all wanted to fuck her and the girls all wanted to fuck her up.

"Who is you?" the teacher frowned looking at her roster to match a name with the troublemaker. Hazel stood, smiled, and drew inspiration from drama class.

"Well, I'm Hazel Sanders. 16, from Sugar Hill, Sugar Hill in Gwinnett that is, not the ghetto one," she said frowning up at the thought.

"Who dis bitch 'posed to be?" a girl named Shanadoa said talking to her cheap sandaled feet.

"Bitch?" Hazel asked indignantly and paid for it instantly.

"Who you calling a bitch? Bitch!" she said crossing the room like weaved lighting.

The wild little ghetto girl was on her ass so fast she didn't know what hit her. Jealous girls always go for the hair and face first. Shanadoa tried to pull a plug out of her hair but the regular salon treatments had it healthy as a horse. The false nail attack on her face was foiled as well. Hazel used her athletic legs to shove the girl across the room. Security rushed in like a prison tactical team and broke it up.

In a school that actually had a murder rate a fight was no big deal. The combatants were taken to their counselor who told them to shake hands and guided them back to class. The word spread like wild fire and by the end of the day, everyone was waiting on a show down.

YOLO

The Lovely Little Lunatic

Chapter 1

"Damn it Philomina, did you have to put these so tight!" Thadeous Frank grumbled straining once more to free himself. His wrist and ankles were secured firmly by thick plastic ties to the heavy dining room chair in the extravagantly furnished dining room. It made no sense complaining to her at the opposite end of the long oak table because she was in the same position.

"She has our baby Thadeous; I did what I was told to do!" his wife shot back in a muted whisper through clenched teeth.

Mrs. Frank wasn't one to sass her husband, especially since he provided her lavish lifestyle. She turned a blind eye to all his indiscretions but had no doubt his insatiable greed was the cause of the current predicament.

Thadeous Frank was about as straight as a circle. In the real world people seek trustworthiness and honesty in a C.P.A. but in the underworld corruption is a virtue. Mr. Frank had a knack for taking duffle bags of dirty, filthy, drug blood money and bringing it back crisp and clean. On average, he ran a hundred mil through his financial washing machine annually. He took a generous ten percent for his trouble. He proved true the adage of no honor among thieves by skimming a few more points off here and there. He didn't have much respect for his black and Latino customers and assumed they wouldn't miss it. Most didn't, however, Casper did. He may have been the boss of the Black Mobb but he was neither black nor stupid. He wrote the first loss off as an oversight the next time the money was short he sent someone to collect.

"Please Thad, give her what she wants! She has our Jacinthia!" Philomina Frank pleaded.

"Look she'll never find it. Never! Once she gets tired of looking I'll give her a few grand from the safe and let her scurry along," he shot back. Baby or no baby he had no plans on coming off that cash. He liked the kid and all, but she wasn't worth ten million to him.

"Please, it's been hours. Jacinthia must be terrified," Mrs. Frank moaned looking at the kitchen door where the intruder took her child.

"Stop bitching, you're making too much out of it. What can that girl do?" he said curtly. Thadeous was smug like that, confident, always in charge. The silly man had no idea who was upstairs in their home searching for stolen monies.

"You're good! I still can't find it!" the intruder sang in the sing-sing manner of an eight year old as she breezed back into the dining room.

The couple both frowned at the sexy maid outfit she had changed into but for different reasons. The high priced item was cut low in front and high enough in back to show her pert caramel ass in a thong underneath. Thadeous recalled the one time his pasty white wife wore it for him and it hadn't look like this.

"Is she wearing my lingerie?" Mrs. Frank complained to her husband then turned to the girl. "Where did you get that?"

"Same place I got this," she giggled and produced a large brown dildo. Brown from the porn star who modeled for it. The white lady turned beet red from embarrassment.

"Well I never!" she huffed indignantly. The intruder frowned dubiously, sniffed the vibrator, and gave it a flick from her tongue.

"Yes you have," the girl giggled sheepishly. She looked at her target and covered her mouth suddenly coy. "Ooh I see you!"

"Thadeous!" Philomina shouted seeing her husband's stubby little erection standing up.

"Here relax," the uninvited guest said turning the knob at the base of the dildo. She giggled again when it began to vibrate with a soft buzz. She shoved it under the woman's vagina and tuned towards the kitchen with Thadeous' eyes glued to her ass.

"How's Jacinthia? She must be hungry," Mrs. Frank asked desperately.

"I doubt it," the girl laughed over her shoulder as she left the room. "We'll talk more after dinner."

"Just give her what she wants! I've said nothing about your affairs and...stuff," she demanded trying to ignore the building pleasure the vibrator was creating.

"She said we'll talk after dinner. She hasn't found anything in the..." he paused to look at the grandfather clock, "four hours she's been her! I'll give her ten grand and she can run off and buy some crack and colorful clothes that niggers love so much!"

Mrs. Frank missed the last sentence from the buzzing between her legs. She shook her head 'no' as she tried in vain to stave off an orgasm. It was futile and she came with a loud grunt. It was the best orgasm she'd had with her husband in the same room. Now she concentrated and went for seconds. Her pleasure was cut short before she got to bust another nut.

"Dinner is served," the girl announced pushing the sterling silver dinner cart into the dining room. On it were two plates topped by silver domes to keep the food warm.

"Would you mind loosening our hands so that we may partake in this wonderful meal?" Mr. Frank requested sweetly. He attempted to hide his devious plan behind the kind words and pasted on smile. The fifty-ish out of shape white man figured he could over-power the little girl. Boy was he wrong.

"Um...ok but one at a time," she relented. Thadeous again watched her firm ass shift as she skipped into the next room.

She returned a few seconds later with the black satchel she came with. Before she opened it, she pulled the blonde dreadlock wig off and stretched her neck in relief. It made a dense thud when she placed it on the table. She un-zipped the bag and pulled out a long chrome pistol and even longer chrome silencer. "In case you try anything"

The girl next pulled a pair of wire snips and danced over to the Mrs. She cut the plastic tie that had broken into her skin from movements. The woman immediately snatched the vibrator from between her legs.

"Ladies first," the server said placing the plate on the table in front of her. She removed the dome with an air of flair complete with, "Ta dah!"

"Oh!" Mrs. Frank uttered at the attractive meal on her good china. She also noticed how pretty the girl was now that her face was no longer obscured by the dreads. She was the exact same shade that the lady took her coffee with milk, not cream. Although her features were delicate and defined, she had an odd look in her eyes. The far-away gaze of a lunatic. The curious gape of the deranged.

"We have wild brown rice with slivers of almond, braised Brussels sprouts in butter-garlic sauce and I'm sorry but I can't pronounce the meat. Jaza or jasm? Something like that," the girl explained.

Philomina was scared the food would be poisoned but she was more afraid of the big pistol on the table. After a second of contemplation, she decided to eat. She popped a whole Brussels sprout in her mouth and chewed. A slow nod of approval began as she savored the flavor. Next, she sampled the rice and finally the pretty kabobs of meat and peppers.

"How's my baby?" Mrs. Frank asked after swallowing.

"You tell me?" the chef asked in return.

"Huh, I don't follow?" she frowned curiously.

"You said how's your baby and I said you tell me. That's what you're eating. I didn't over cook her did I?"

"Noooo!" the mother screamed as the nightmare was multiplied times infinity. She pulled and tugged at the plastic tie cutting deeply into her wrist. "You're sick! Sick!"

"Me? You're the one who ate her baby lady," the girl shot back sarcastically. With the woman busy trying to cut her own hand off she turned her attention to Mr. Frank. "Have some? It's thigh, I hear that's the best part. I wouldn't know cuz I don't eat kids. Well..."

"Mm mm!" Thadeous declined squeezing his mouth tight and moving his head from side to side to avoid the fork full of baby thigh meat she extended.

"Ooh, I know what will make you open up," she exclaimed cheerfully at her bright idea. She grabbed the gun and fired a silent round into his calf. Harmless, but it got him to open his mouth wide in an opera worthy high note.

"Good?" she asked shoving the meat inside his open mouth. She didn't wait for an answer and went back into her black bag. Thadeous took the opportunity to spit his kid onto the marble floor.

Both Franks were dealing with their problems but the next item out of the bag took precedence. She stopped thrashing about and he longer felt the burn of the gunshot.

"What the hell is that?" Thadeous demanded as if its mere presence offended him. Actually, it should.

"This," she began, holding up the circular wire contraption, "it's the D.C. 2000! That's short for decapitator 2000. I saw it in a movie and had to have it!"

She went on to explain how the spring-loaded wire hoop snapped shut to a zero circumference when activated. It was strong enough to cut through a 2x4 so skin and bones were no problem at all.

"Now I'm going to cut both of your heads off," she said plainly, as if it were no big deal.

"Why both of our heads? I didn't have anything to do with any of this!" Mrs. Frank pleaded in an attempt to save herself.

"No, both of his heads I meant," the girl explained going back into the satchel. The garden shears she produced needed no explanation.

"Wait! Wait! Wait!" Thadeous appealed as she approached. "I'll tell you where the money is!"

"Too late," said slipping the D.C. 2000 over his head. "I'm glad you didn't give it to me."

"Go to hell!" he shouted and in a final act of defiance he spit in her face. The lovely little lunatic smiled, licked the saliva from around her mouth, and picked up his flaccid penis.

"Ok, bye-bye," she sang and simultaneous hit the switch and closed the shears. The tiny dick head popped off and rolled under his chair. A second later, his big, bald head fell into his lap.

Mrs. Frank looked on in stunned silence as her husband was decapitated. Whoever the girl was, she was a killer. A killa, a real animal. She let out a sigh of contentment and accepted her fate.

"Well, time to go with your baby, but don't tell her you ate her," she whispered conspiratorially.

Mrs. Frank lifted her chin prepaid to die with dignity. Instead of shooting her or cutting any parts off, the girl prepared to leave. She packed her pistol and D.C. 2000 into the bag along with the shears. She took the wire cutters into the kitchen and cut the gas line leading to the restaurant size stove. Then breezed back through the dining room ignoring the confused woman.

The girl made a stop in the family room and lit the fireplace. Once the gas made it this far the house would be leveled by the explosion. A sly smile spread over her face as she stepped over the body of the butler. He had smiled brightly when he opened the door for her and she shot him in it.

When she got into her SUV and drove away, she added the two kills to her tally. The total was now 99 and she wasn't quite 21. She pulled her cell phone out to report in to her boss. Casper smiled brightly when he saw the name on his caller ID.

"Yolo! Did you get it?" the white boss of the Black Mobb asked eagerly. He didn't need the money but didn't want anyone to have the satisfaction of stealing from him and enjoying it.

"No, he wouldn't tell me," she replied sadly. "Good news though. The D.C. 2000 works like a charm!"

"That is good news. Have fun?" Casper inquired.

"I did. I did," Yolo said bouncing in her seat.

A thunderous roar rocked the SUV and shook the earth. A glance in the rearview mirror showed a huge orange fireball where the house once stood.

"Yay! One Hundred!" she cheered knowing Mrs. Frank was in the debris blown sky high.

You may wonder why a girl would derive such joy from killing people and the answer is because she's crazy. You may also wonder how she amassed such a high body count at such a young age. The answer to that is simple too; she started early.

Yung Pimpin
prologue

An evil smirk twisted Yung Pimpin's otherwise handsome face as he spotted his target. The notorious Sammy the pimp was posted up at the bar talking loud and dressed even louder. He was old school to death in a yellow three-piece suit complete with yellow gators and a yellow hat, with one long yellow feather extending from it. He couldn't help but wonder for a second if it was actually some place in nature where yellow alligators or ostriches thrived; perhaps some gay ass enchanted swamp with bullfrogs giving each other blowjobs. But now wasn't the time to ponder over it, now was the time to kill.

Yung Pimpin represented the new era in pimpin'. Instead of finger waves like his target, he wore an intricate array of braids running down to his shoulders. A fresh white wife beater showed off his lean muscular frame decorated with colorful tats. A diamond-laden 'YP' medallion hung to the middle of his chest from a diamond-crusted platinum chain. Expensive designer jeans slung low on his waist sat on top of exclusive sneakers.

The patrons of the speedy after hours' club grew quiet at the arrival of the highly anticipated showdown. Rumors of the battle had the P&H bar filled to capacity. The joint was named after proprietors Paul and Harold 20 years ago but those who know, knew P&H now stood for pimps and hoes. This was Ground Zero, Pimp Central, and Hoe Headquarters.

The sudden change in the air put Sammy the pimp on high alert. It was that eerie calm before the storm. The look in the soulless eyes of his bottom bitch confirmed the danger. There is no honor among thieves so the honorable thing would be for Yung Pimpin to bash the back of his head in then go shoot a game of pool until the cops came. No sense running because, again, there's no honor among thieves and someone was going to snitch on him.

"Heard you was looking for me," Yung demanded, tapping the man on the shoulder, making two mistakes at once. The first was talking instead of swinging and the second was touching instead of swinging. He paid for them both at the same time.

"I am!" Sammy said as he whirled around and swung. The open hand slap sounded like a thunderclap when it connected. A slap stings enough on its own but the razorblade concealed in his fingers made it burn. The slap was designed to humiliate but the blade served a more sinister purpose.

"Pimp fight!" a broke down old hoe named Debbie announced with glee. Her raspy voice had a slight echo from years of cum shots knocking out her tonsils. Her black lips where shaped in a perfect 'O' from all the dicks sucked. They looked like an old tire on her worn face.

The only thing better than a ho fight was a pimp fight and this bar had seen its share of both. Pimps when they do fight, fight to the death. Be the death literal or figurative, somebody had to die. Even if the loser lives, there will be no more pimpin' for him around here. Lose a pimp fight and your stable and respect is transferred to the winner. To the victor goes the spoils and in this case the bootie is the actual booty. Pardon the oxymoron but no self-respecting ho will whore for a pimp who gets punked.

"Get him daddy," Sammy's bottom bitch hissed like the snake she was.

Coming from her, it was another slap in the face and made Yung Pimpin hesitate. That hesitation cost him another slap in the face by the older pimp. This one was a Venus Williams backhand formally known as the pimp slap. It was the ultimate in disrespect. Even pimps don't like to be pimp slapped.

"Miss that good Wet-Wet don't you boy?" Sammy teased.

"You can take that bitch to hell with you," Yung snarled. He knew if he won, she would be his again. This time he would do what he should have done many times over; kill her.

Yung lifted his hand to his face and felt the blood. The hand then turned into a fist and threw a straight jab that popped the pimp in his slick talking mouth. It was quickly reciprocated by a two-piece.

Both men shared the same height and weight among other things. The DJ cut the music and hit the lights so no one would miss the action. Camera phones began filming; this was going to be on world star.

"They kind of favor each other?" a young whore said with a curious frown.

"They should, they father and son," Wet-Wet reported. She should know; she was part of the problem. It really wasn't about her but then again it was.

The pugnacious patriarch and progeny pimps went back and forth trading blows. The fight was pretty evenly matched with both lumped up and bloody when the inevitable happened.

Just like male Rams run full speed into each other with their horns and giraffes use their long necks to fight, pimps use straight razors. Once they got tired of punching, out came the blades.

"You know how to use that?" Sammy taunted and took a swipe.

The blow opened the front of Yung Pimpin's shirt and sliced into his skin. The pain reminded him of the pistol in his pocket. He answered the question when he swung back, opening a similar hole in his father's yellow jacket.

Back and forth, blow for bloody blow, the father and son battled. It wasn't a battle of good versus evil, more like evil against more evil. You'll have to hear the whole story to determine which one was which.

Getting nowhere with the razors suddenly both Parker pimps pulled pistols. Only one got off a shot. One died, the other killed, again.

STUD 1, 2, 3, & 4

When I got in from the robbery, I just wanted to crash. Murder always made me sleepy. There was my mother, up in the middle of the night, praying as usual. Unless she was on her period, Laylah spent half the night praying. She would chant in Arabic in a soft, melodic tone. I'd heard it so much that I knew half the words to the one she said most often: "Bis-millaahir Rahman-nir Raheem..." Most nights, she paid me no attention if I came in when she prayed, but this time, she cut it short as I walked in.

As she did her closeout from right to left, I saw the reason for the truncated prayer. There, on the coffee table, was my strap-on, and right next to it was my growing DVD porn collection!

My first instinct was to run. I turned to bolt out the door, but her words held me in place.

What shocked me most was her tone. She was eerily calm. "Wait. Come sit down," she ordered in a subdued tone, yet making it clear it was not optional. "Well, I guess it's more than just a fad. I guess you won't just grow out of it," she mused, pushing the sex toy with a finger.

"Ma, it's—"

"Chill, Andrea. I can smell the thing from here." She frowned, shaking her head. "Your girlfriend needs a bath."

I shook my head, thinking about Tameka's nasty ass. There was nothing to say, so I said nothing. There was no need to anyway because her next words said all that needed saying.

"Good and evil cannot coexist in the same place," she stated helplessly.

"What does that mean?" I asked, exasperated.

"You have to leave. Please return to what—or to who—kept you to three a.m. You can collect your things whenever," she sighed.

I was too tired to argue, so I shrugged and got up to leave.

"Keys please," my mother said, extending her open palm.

I tossed the whole ring to her and walked out. A quick hop down a flight of stairs later and I was ringing Ramel's doorbell.

What Readers are Saying...

TOTALLY AWESOME!!!!
This story is great! The suspense, the drama, the
plots...oh how I love this author! He is truly the
best in a league of his own. He brings books to
life making it seem like you're right in the middle
of the action. With everything surrounding
the plots there's still a humor that makes his books
fantastic!
SO LOVED THIS BOOK
AND ALL OTHERS BY SA'ID. IF YOU ARE NOT
FAMILIAR GET FAMILIAR WITH THIS AUTHOR!
YOU WILL NOT BE DISAPPOINTED BY ANY OF
THE BOOKS SO CLICK ALL NOW AND ENJOY
SOME GREAT READS.

A MUST READ
I Love this author and this is
one of the best reads.
If I buy one of Sa'id's books, I can't put it down until I
get to the end and then I'm looking for the next
one.
Must Buy
Omfg i love u Sa'id! Your pen game is on 100!
I'm just glad you never got wack wit ur writing
unlike a lot of authors
The Man with the Golden Pen
This book was just what I expected from this
Author. His pen game is phenomenal and it's
like his ink is gold because his books are
always on point. This man is a beast when it comes to writing. He
had me laughing through the whole book.

Loved It!!!!

Sa'id Salaam is always on top of his game
when it comes to writing!!!!! With anything
that you pick up from him you will be
intrigued throughout the whole book!!!!

A Good Read!

I love this Author, everything I have read by
him was good, including this. All his books
contain a message, sex, money, and comedy.

Great read!!

I always enjoy reading a book from Sa`id.
Always full of adventure and always up to
date. Great book. I want more!!!

Fantastic

I love this book the author is the most
amazing storyteller I have ever read.

BEAST!

I absolutely adore Sa'id
Salaam!! I just don't know how many ways I
can say his talent is astounding. I don't
wanna sound repetitive, I read & review ALL
his books!! Why?? Because he is an absolute
KILLA with the pen!